PROC
James Morja

MORFASSON
Ubi Tenebris Cadit Surgent Mos Fabulam

This book is a work of fiction. Although many of the places mentioned are real, the people within them are not. Any resemblance to real people, living or dead, is purely coincidental.

This Edition ©James Morfa/Churchill-2024

THE ARCHER OF EASTGATE

It is never realistic. Murder I mean. Fictional murder. Even those shows and books which *claim* to be realistic don't come close to anything real. The writers overcomplicate things and blow everything into ridiculous proportions. They throw in a slew of murders (usually three) and include a long, drawn out search to find a killer who, it turns out, was right under the nose of the detective the entire time.

That self-same detective misses an important clue and they won't find it until the end. At that point they'll instantly work out who did it, as though it were obvious all along. You can guarantee that the murderer will disappear from the story for a while, just so that the writer can throw in a few red herrings.

Real murder investigations are simpler. Some would go so far as to say boring. In most cases we know who did it inside of a few hours. Most of the time, *most*, there is only *one* murder. We police never take our eyes off a suspect until we are absolutely one hundred percent certain that they're innocent. There is no disappearing for a while in a real murder investigation.

What irritates me most?

The way *the detectives* behave. They spend their entire careers solving a black parade of insane murders with some dimwitted sidekick trailing two steps behind asking idiot questions. Nowhere in the world does any detective have that many murders in their career. Most cops are lucky to even get one murder.

Oh, and at the end of each case their murderer will throw themselves under a bus or off a building or something.

There's always some dysfunction going on. The detective is a maverick or has an alcohol problem or is divorced and never sees his daughter or some such malarkey.

Ok, I know more than my fair share of divorced cops. That's to be expected. Policing is a rough job. I have been divorced for over sixteen years now but I (and most others) don't let my relationships play into my work and I've always made time for Corwen, my son. I've always put him before the job and if there is one thing I can say with absolute certainty it is that I am not dysfunctional. In *no way* am I dysfunctional. I don't know any cop who is either.

I threw the remote down. Angry. After going through nearly five hundred channels I had found nothing I wanted to watch and in the process of finding fudge I had come across an extraordinarily large amount of those aforementioned crime dramas. More than normal for a Tuesday night. All variations on the above. I'm even sure there were two different adaptations of the same *Miss Marple* story playing on two different channels.

Glanced at the clock. Eleven. Almost.

If I went to bed now then it might be possible for me to drift into a deep enough sleep so as not to be woken when Corwen clattered through the front door with some random he'd picked up. This would be followed by a sexualised Shakespeare misquote. Something cringe along the lines of: 'Let me give you the stuff that dreams are made of.' Then they would begin eighty minutes of raucous intercourse. I was always, weekly, twice weekly sometimes, having to apologise to the neighbours and, personally, that sound always disgusted me. I'm not a prude or anything like that. Sex is natural and the desire to have sex is only human but I *don't* want to hear anybody else doing it, let alone my own son. Sex should be an intimate, personal experience. It should happen behind closed doors. Quietly. Nobody else should know about it.

I have had many words with Corwen about this over the breakfast table. None of them have ever done any good, alas.

He must get his sexual prowess from his mother's side of the family. They are *all* loud and promiscuous. I still shudder whenever I recall the wedding night of Corwen's cousin when there were six of them (and their partners) all going at it at the same time- Seven men and five women. Not all in the same room thankfully. Fair to say that I hadn't slept that night and nor, from the sound of it, had anybody else.

Pushing whatever Corwen was getting up to from my mind I went to bed. I had a book on the sideboard, a Catherine Cookson, but I wasn't in a mood for reading. Switched out the light and threw myself against the pillow, feeling my limbs ease and every muscle give their nightly cry of late middle-age agony.

By the time I lifted my head again it was gone one o'clock and I could hear a valley's accent in the hallway asking: 'Are these your tits I see before me, their nipps towards my hand?' Far from Corwen's best. It was one of his worst. I wondered if her name was Beth.

That wasn't what had awoken me. It was the phone on the sideboard. Bleating. Yelling that I was required at a road traffic accident across town. Either that or someone in Nigeria was trying to defraud me with claims that I had inherited a dukedom.

"If you've rang to say I've inherited a dukedom I don't want it," I said, leaving the phone by my ear to make sure the call wasn't important. It was.

"Sorry Proctor, no dukedom tonight. Just a dead man outside the Grosvenor." It was my D.C.I, Gareth Thomlinson.

"What's up Gov?"

"Like I said. Dead man outside the Grosvenor. Come as soon as you're awake."

The buzz at the other end told me that Thomlinson had hung up.

Yesterday's clothes would do for the time being. I could dress properly in the morning when whatever business outside the Grosvenor had concluded. It wouldn't take long.

Brewed myself a coffee to perk myself up, taking it all in one go, and climbed into my *Infiniti G37 Convertible,* the car I had bought during my so called mid-life crisis.

It may not have been to everybody's taste, even Corwen hated it and derogatorily referred to it as 'the Nissan,' but I liked the thing. It was a good driver and there was plenty of leg room.

Putting the top down I set the gear box to manual and was soon well on my way to the city with the sounds of the Bee-Gees flowing from the speaker system.

A mile and ten minutes after setting off I rolled up in front of the *Disney Store* with '*Tragedy*' blaring out from the speakers. Perhaps it was not the best thing to have been playing in hindsight. I don't really care. It was just a song and it harmed no one. As I made my way towards the police cordon set up across Eastgate the two uniforms patrolling it raised their eyebrows and looked at each other with a coy smile.

"What have we got?" I snapped, passing under the cordon.

"Businessman. Dewi Croft, sarge. Shot from behind with an arrow, sometime just after midnight."

"Christ!" I blasphemed. That was all I needed. A homicide on my beat.

Passed under the wall and saw the SOCOs buzzing about outside the Grosvenor. Thomlinson waved to me from the pavement and as I approached he silently pointed to the ground.

Lying face down, half on and half off the pavement, was a man in his mid-forties. Bald. Neck of many folds. From the small of his back protruded a green and black fletched arrow, embedded at an angle of forty five degrees.

I looked in the direction he had been facing and then turned around. The trajectory of the arrow was clear.

Whoever shot this man had shot Mr Croft from *on top of* the wall.

"Dewi Croft. Forty three from Wrecsam. Owns a media publishing company down there. *Iard-Ysgubor Cyhoeddi.* They run *Cymraeg Magazine* and a few others."

"I think it's quite obvious what happened here. Some fool took a disliking to him or something he's published and decided to take a pot shot at him from the wall."

"A little more than that I'm afraid," Thomlinson said. "The M.O fits with a certain urban legend."

"Urban legend?"

"You know the one? No? About how it's legal to shoot a Welshman with a bow and arrow within the city walls after midnight?"

It sounded ridiculous and quite untrue.

"That isn't true is it? Please tell me it isn't true!" If it *were* true we were up shit creek. How could we bring in a killer who was *protected* by the law? Didn't get a direct answer to my question. Thomlinson only shrugged.

"What about witnesses? Who found the body?"

"No witnesses to the murder, so far as we know. Body

was found by Elsie MacGonagall. Works the concierge desk. She's waiting for us in the lobby."

"Good. Anybody been up to the wall yet?"

"Only to close it off."

"We'll check up there first. Leave the girl to sweat for a bit longer. Could be she's guilty." Even though she had found the body I wasn't ruling her out as a suspect. Everybody is possibly guilty until they're definitively proven innocent.

The nearest access point to the wall was down a narrow alley between the edge of the Grosvenor and *S. S Milton*, the pawnbrokers. Few people used this access point. Everyone used the stairs on the other side. Even *I* hadn't known about it until Corwen pointed it out on a shopping excursion the previous Christmas. One thing I noticed whilst down there, through the gloom of the night, was that there was no service door into the hotel. There was a wooden panel where there had once been a door but it didn't open. Made certain in my mind the idea that anybody leaving the hotel would have come out of the front door.

"If the killer was the girl then it's likely she'll have come down from the wall this way before 'discovering' the body," Thomlinson suggested.

"If she knows about it of course."

"If she works at the Grosvenor she'll *have* to know about it. Not only is it right next to the hotel but as a concierge the management will expect her to know the city inside and out." It stood to reason but I wasn't convinced.

We turned left towards the clock tower above the road. Nothing out of the ordinary anywhere. Clock was lit, usually was at night, and the street below was silent apart from the SOCOs looking for flowers of evidence. There was nothing around the wall which suggested foul play or that anything untoward had happened. Had it not been for the SOCOs or the body of Dewi Croft lying in the street you could have been forgiven for thinking that it was any other night.

I examined the railings directly in front of the body. The bolt *must* have been fired from here but the railings were high, coming up to my chin, so the killer must have either been exceptionally tall or kneeling down. I went onto one knee and looked through at the body.

"Do you think that somebody could fire an arrow *through* these railings?" Thomlinson knelt down next to me.

"All you'd need would be to place your bow close enough to get the arrow through."

"We should be able to find out how tall this person was from the trajectory of the arrow. How tall do you think Dewi Croft was?"

"Five eight I should imagine." I concurred, concluded that the arrow was embedded in his back at three feet four. The body was set back from the wall at around one hundred and forty nine feet. My two respective firing heights meanwhile, at the top and bottom of the railings, were sixty two and seventy four feet off the ground. That meant that the arrow had either travelled seventy six feet or eighty six feet.

That sounds a lot but you have to remember that a proper expert archer can fire a bolt some five hundred yards, one and a half thousand feet, which is far more than I was dealing with. And let us not forget that our murderer was firing downwards, which meant that his target would be easier to hit.

If the archer had fired the arrow at eighty six feet from the ground that meant the angle of the shot would have been somewhere in the region of twenty seven degrees.

That didn't seem right, judging by the positioning of the arrow.

I calculated that from a low firing position the angle of shot would have been between fifty and fifty five degrees. More like it

"Whoever did this shot from low down. I'm certain."

"Pity," Thomlinson mourned. "If he'd shot from the top then we'd have an easier collar. We'd be looking for someone over six foot."

I considered more about how this crime might have been committed.

The first thing a killer usually does after committing a murder is dispose of the weapon. From here there were two fast routes to places where the weapon could easily be disposed of, both along the walls. I disregarded an escape from Eastgate or its environs as any fool knows that carrying a crossbow (or similar) through the streets looks suspicious.

Gazing in either direction along the wall I saw that both feasible options of escape were dimly lit. Only a few lamps set apart at large distances. One way led towards the amphitheatre and the river. I immediately assumed that this was *not* the way our killer had escaped. There were the steps over Newgate for one thing. They could be fatal, even if you weren't in a hurry. There was no other entry point (that wouldn't be locked off) on the walls between the clock and the other side of Newgate so if our killer *had* ran that way he would have had to cross it. That was too dangerous a thing to attempt at night *and* in a hurry. Nobody who knew the city would have ran that way.

Then there was the river itself. The killer would have to go a fair way along the wall before they could get down to that level and dispose of the weapon.

That distance was too far for my liking.

The second possible escape route ran north, past the cathedral and towards the canal. A more likely prospect. It was a flat stretch and the northern city wall ran almost parallel to the edge of the canal. It would take no great amount of effort to toss something over the side and into the water. There was no doubt in my mind that somewhere at that end would also be where the killer had left the walls. There were plenty of exits up that way, many more than by Newgate. Where the killer had gone afterwards required some more thought but it would not be impossible to figure out.

"How soon can we get someone to dive the canal?" I asked, heading back towards the steps.

"First thing in the morning. If the weapon is in there it won't take us long to find it."

Thomlinson and I share similar processes. We both look at the situation before us and make our deductions based on the simplest solution to the problem. Ninety five percent of the time we are right with our first guesses and the other five percent of the time we are almost there.

Most criminals, despite what crime writers would have you believe, are not masterminds. They're mostly idiots who only *think* they're clever. They rarely think properly about what they're doing. They just assume they'll get away with it. Ergo, it's usually the case that they take only the most basic of steps to cover up their misdemeanours.

Take our archery assassin. He may have thought that in the dark of the walls nobody would be able to work out which way he had escaped. He may have thought nobody could or *would* see him. However, he never assumed that any half-idiot policeman would know that after committing a premeditated murder the first thing someone does is try and cover up the crime. The assassin may have thought he was being clever, using the walls to escape and dispose of the weapon, but it was an obvious and logical thing to do. Further still, he may have thought we wouldn't know which end of the wall he disposed of the weapon but that too could be logically deduced.

If on the slight chance that the weapon turned out not to be in the canal we would still know the direction in which he had escaped. There was only one other place he could dispose of it so quickly. And once his direction of escape was deduced we could easily establish where he had gone. Tracing someone in the modern world, even if they don't want to be found, is not difficult. This is true of murderers in the extreme.

Reaching the street Thomlinson and I brushed away the

SOCOs and swept through the main doors of the Grosvenor. The whole place stinks of Nuevo-riche pretension and sports stars who get paid a fortune for kicking a ball around and get to retire at thirty three. It's all pomp and self-indulgence. Not my type of place at all. The foyer has no windows, except in the door, and yet it is vastly over lit by an array of down lighters and table lamps.

A hive of white suede chairs are placed randomly about the place.

It was in one of these chairs I found Elsie MacGonagall. A young thing with black hair and green eyes streaked with tears and running mascara. She didn't much look like someone who was capable of cold blooded murder. Then again they never do.

Myself and Thomlinson sat down.

"Miss MacGonagall? I'm D.S Simon Proctor and this is my colleague, D.C.I Gareth Thomlinson. We'd like to ask you a few questions."

Elsie dabbed at her eyes with a tissue.

"I don't want to talk about it. But I suppose that if you have to ask your questions…"

"We don't *have* to Miss MacGonagall. We *must*. We *must* because we have to a catch a killer." Thomlinson's tone was abrasive. Not good for speaking to someone who has just found a corpse in the street. Not good even if she was a suspect.

"I thought it was legal to kill a Welshman after dark?"

"So you know the man who was killed?"

"Yes. He's staying here with his wife Mirabel. He came to the desk at around midnight to say he was going for a walk and he would be back in a half an hour."

"Did he say where he was going?" Elsie shook her head. "Was there anything unusual about him when he left? Anything you thought suspicious?"

"No. He was just a businessman going out for a late night walk. Why would there be anything suspicious about that?"

"For all we know he may have been going to meet someone and that person may have killed him afterwards. It wouldn't be the first time someone was killed over a shady business deal." Elsie screwed up her face.

"Mr Croft wasn't that sort of businessman. He was nice. He was friendly."

"So you spoke to him properly? You had a conversation?"

"I chatted to him before he went for his walk."

"When did Mr Croft arrive at the hotel?"

"This afternoon. He was staying until Friday."

"If he only arrived today how do you know he 'wasn't that sort of businessman,' as you put it?"

Elsie flustered in her seat.

"I... I... He... He flirted with me. He offered to take me out for a stroll under the moonlight. It wasn't dirty old man flirting though. It was nice flirting. The sort all men do when they meet a pretty girl."

"You didn't answer our question, Miss MacGonagall. How do you know he wasn't that sort of businessman?"

"He didn't *seem* like that kind of businessman. He *seemed* nice and friendly."

"So you liked him flirting with you?"

"I was flattered. What girl doesn't like to be asked to go for a stroll in the moonlight?" I again decided it best not to answer her question.

"How did you come across the body, Miss MacGonagall?"

"I had taken my break early and gone out to buy cigarettes. When I came back I saw that Mr Croft was lying dead in the street."

"Where did you go to buy these cigarettes?"

"A newsagents on Northgate street. Opposite King Street."

"Do you have a receipt?"

Elsie reached into her pocket. The reciept confirmed her story. What was interesting about it was that it was time stamped at *12:34*, several minutes *after* Dewi Croft was due back from his walk.

"What time did you leave the hotel to buy cigarettes?"

"It was about twenty five past twelve." She seemed certain of that fact. *Too* certain.

"And you saw nothing suspicious in the street when you left the hotel?"

"If by suspicious you mean did I see a body lying on the pavement then no I didn't."

Elsie was becoming narked and irritable so I eased up on my questioning to make her more comfortable.

"Did you pass anybody on the way there or on the way

back?"

"No. No I didn't."

"What did you do when you saw the body? What did you think?"

"At first I thought it was some drunk fool who'd tumbled out of one of the pubs. Then I remembered most of them close early on a Tuesday night. The only place still open at that time is *Rosies* and people don't start coming out of there until half two on a Tuesday night... That's when I saw the arrow in his back and recognised him as Mr Croft."

"And then what did you do Miss MacGonagall?"

"I did what anybody would do. I screamed."

I heard Thomlinson give a subtle sigh of sarcastic despair.

"What was the result of this scream?" Stupid question.

"It brought out some of the hotel staff. My relief at the concierge desk. Wendy her name is. She brought me back inside whilst one of the night porters, Cole Spencer, called the police and waited outside until you arrived."

"How many people work nights at the hotel, Miss MacGonagall?"

"It depends on the number of guests. We're not too full at

the moment so there are only five of us at night."

"How often are staff required to work the night shift?"

"Six nights a month and then as required," Elsie answered curtly.

"Do you think any of the other night staff could have killed Mr Croft?"

"I don't think so. I don't know how they could have done. I can't see why they *would*."

"And what about any of the guests? Did anyone else go outside other than Mr Croft?" Elsie racked her brains for a while before shaking her head, an act that seemed suspicious given her next answer.

"Mrs Croft went outside for a cigarette at around quarter past twelve but she came back inside just as I was leaving."

That sounded very interesting, especially given how Mrs Croft had apparently 'come back inside' as Elsie was leaving. Did she really come back inside or did she just pretend?

That was a question for later so I stored it.

"What about archery Miss MacGonagall? Ever tried your hand?" Elsie looked shocked.

"Are you saying that *I* killed Mr Croft? Because if you are you're wrong. I *didn't* do it."

"We have to ask these questions Miss MacGonagall, if only to eliminate you from our inquiries," Thomlinson said.

Elsie wriggled in her chair.

"I did try archery once. My boyfriend wanted to try it when we were on holiday and he dragged me to it. I wasn't very good though."

That was all the questions I needed to ask for the moment so I stood up from my chair. Then I thought of something else.

"Where are the nearest steps onto the wall Miss MacGonagall?" She looked at me as though I were mad but answered anyway.

"There's one down the side of the hotel and another on the opposite side of the road next to the shoe shop."

I nodded my thanks and walked away towards the lift with Thomlinson following me.

"What do you think?" Thomlinson asked.

"It's possible. She could have left the hotel, climbed up to the walls and shot Dewi Croft. Then she could have ran along the walls to the canal, disposed of the weapon and got off at Northgate to go into the newsagents to provide herself with an alibi. But then again… Where would she hide the weapon in the meantime? She can't have brought it into work with her without being noticed. What would her motive be if Croft only arrived this afternoon? The flirting? But if it was a spur of the moment thing like that then where on earth did she get the weapon from at such short notice? No. She doesn't make any sense as the killer." Thomlinson didn't sound convinced by my reasoning.

"She had the opportunity. She was outside the hotel at the time Croft was returning and, as you say, her escape route was able to feed into her alibi."

"There isn't a lot of time though is there? Only nine minutes between leaving the hotel and buying the cigarettes at the newsagents. It would take her half of that time to run up to Northgate alone, let alone shoot Croft as well."

"She may not have left the hotel when she said she did," Thomlinson snorted.

We arrived at the third floor and one of the presidential suites. Thomlinson knocked four times and we entered into something more like a luxury apartment than a hotel room. It was painted a white to yellow colour that seemed to me to be off and all the fittings were covered by a faux-Japanese floral pattern.

Hideous.

We passed through a small hallway and then came into a sitting room where Mirabel Croft was rigidly poised on a sofa, looking down her nose at a uniform.

Mrs Croft was mutton. That kind of woman who grows up with no money and tries to pretend she's wealthier than she is by slathering herself with too much cheap makeup and hair bleach. Of course, Mrs Croft *was* now wealthy but that hadn't stopped her from continuing to slather herself in too much cheap makeup and rinsing her head in a sink full of bleach once a month. This was all despite the fact that she was approaching forty five and should have been long past the stage where too much makeup and hair bleach are even a consideration.

I could see that she had also had botox. Her face had that peculiar, unmoveable plastic sheen you get from such things. She was very much a *WAG* kind of woman, if you understand my meaning.

"Mrs Croft? I'm D.S Proctor and this is D.C.I Thomlinson. Do you mind if we ask you some questions about your husband?" Mirabel Croft nodded her approval and we sat down whilst the uniform dismissed herself to another room.

"If you think I killed him for his money I didn't," she told us instantly. Hers was the most grating scouse accent and it shot right through me despite the fact that I am, myself, a scouser and quite used to that kind of accent.

"Why would we think *you* killed him Mrs Croft?"

"I saw the way you both looked at me when you sat down. You thought I was guilty and you're determined to prove it."

"We're police officers Mrs Croft. We aren't paid to think. We're paid to collect evidence and arrest whoever committed the crime. Now, if you wouldn't mind answering our questions?" Mrs Croft snorted and folded her arms. "Why did you and your husband come to Chester Mrs Croft?"

"Tomorrow was our twentieth wedding anniversary. Dewi

was treating me to a weekend away."

"Was that your only reason for coming here?"

"No," she pished. "Dewi was looking into acquiring the *Deva Gazette.* He had a lunch meeting with the editor and a tour of the offices before we checked in."

"What did you do whilst he was touring the offices?"

"I went shopping, of course." Mrs Croft said that as though it were obvious.

"Did you buy anything? An anniversary present for your husband?" Mrs Croft nodded.

"I bought him a set of platinum cuff links. They're in a drawer in the study." Thomlinson went to take a look.

"Did you buy anything else Mrs Croft? Perhaps jewellery for yourself or an ornament or something to excite your love life?" Mrs Croft laughed loudly.

"Excite my love life? No! Dewi was a prude. He wouldn't stand for anything like that. Sex with him was like fucking a log. He insisted on doing it in the dark, under the covers with no foreplay and no movement. I mean can you imagine? No movement!"

"Have you ever slept with anyone other than your

husband?"

"Not whilst we've been married. That's not lady like. I did have a previous boyfriend who did me a couple of times. He was wild. Have you ever had wild sex detective?"

"Yes," I replied bluntly, not going into detail about how Anna had been like a thing possessed when it came to such matters.

Thomlinson returned with the cuff links and I examined them. They were high quality and not something someone might buy if they were planning to off their husband.

"Did you and your husband have any children Mrs Croft?" Once again she laughed something hysterical.

"God no! Dewi wouldn't stand for it. He said it would be a constant reminder of having sex!"

"Did you *want* children? Did you and Mr Croft argue over this?"

"Yes. We argued about it this afternoon. When we came back here after dinner as it happened."

"Where did you dine, if I may be so impertinent to ask that question?"

"*The Boathouse* down by the river. We had a more

expensive restaurant booked for our anniversary tomorrow."

"If you wanted children, Mrs Croft why didn't you adopt or foster? It's very easy these days, I hear. There's even surrogacy." Corwen's cousin Marco and his partner Issac were planning it.

"Dewi still wouldn't hear of it. He hated kiddies and he wouldn't even agree to adopt one."

"How badly would you say you wanted a child Mrs Croft?"

"I'm not getting any younger. My womb's going to shrivel up any day now and I would like to have at least *one* kiddy before it happens."

"I don't believe the menopause causes the womb to actually shrivel up, Mrs Croft!"

"Do you have kiddies detective?" Mrs Croft questioned impertinently.

"Only one and he was quite enough for me!"

"We'll your wife is lucky…"

"Ex-wife," I corrected.

"Ex-wife then. She's lucky. She doesn't have to worry

about what's going to happen to her body because she's already done what she's biologically supposed to do."

"So you believe that it's a woman's duty to have children?"

"As many as she can! A good woman should be popping out a baby at least once every two or three years." I felt the whole feminist movement shifting backwards by a century or two.

Most women I know would have coshed Mrs Croft about the head for what she had just said. My ex-wife certainly *would* have done. In her opinion babies were an unfortunate by-product of sex. As you can probably therefore guess, it was Corwen who played a major role in our divorce. Some of it was also down to my job as a police officer, but it was mostly Corwen.

Anyway, back to feminism... I don't mind feminism. In fact I am all for it in most cases.

"Why did you continue to stay with your husband if you wanted a child Mrs Croft? Why not divorce him and marry someone else?"

"I absolutely *couldn't* marry someone else... NO!" Mrs

Croft sounded as though she were offended by my suggestion. "I *loved* Dewi. He may have been a prude and crap in bed but he was a romantic gentleman and he knew how to treat me like a lady. You can't say that about many men. And besides... Imagine the stain on my reputation that a divorce would cause!"

"Did your husband flirt a lot? I understand he was flirting with the concierge before he left the hotel."

"He was *always* flirting. Flirting was his way of being nice... He liked flirting so long as it didn't go anywhere."

"So you didn't mind it?"

"No. Why would I? I knew that nothing would ever come of it because he was so prudish." I thought that this was rather a naïve view of things. What if something really had come of that flirting? What if he ended up having an affair? What if he was just prudish around *her*?

"Do you think your husband loved you Mrs Croft?"

"Of course he did. What a silly question," Mrs Croft sniffed.

"So tell me then, what happened after the two of you had argued?"

"I believe my husband went to calm himself in the bar downstairs."

"And what time did he come back to the room?"

"Around nine. He watched television for a while and then decided he would go for a short walk before bed."

"And that was around midnight?"

"Yes. It was."

"Did he say where he was going?"

"No he didn't."

"Did he often take late night walks Mrs Croft?" I only received a vague response of 'sometimes.'

"What did you do whilst he went out for his walk Mrs Croft?" I already, in theory, knew the answer to this question but I still asked it in order to gauge her reaction. If she answered that she stayed in her room or even inside the hotel it increased the chances of her guilt. By denying that she was outside it would have told me that she had something to hide.

"I went outside for a cigarette. They don't let you smoke in the hotel." So she wasn't denying she was outside? Nothing to make her look guilty then.

"I should think not," I decried. "Did you see anybody else leave the hotel whilst you were outside smoking?"

"I saw the night porter leaving as I was lighting up but nobody else." That was curious… Elsie MacGonagall had stated that she had left the hotel for her cigarettes during the time Mrs Croft had been outside smoking. Surely she saw her?

"What about the concierge, Elsie MacGonagall. She claims that she left the hotel at around twenty five past twelve. Did you see her leave at any point?"

"The concierge? No. She left the hotel at the same time as I did and I didn't see her return either."

"And what time was this?"

"Around quarter past." Different to what MacGonagall told me. I could easily check the hotel CCTV to see who was telling the truth on the time Elsie MacGonagall left the hotel, so I let the question lie.

"Which way did Miss Macgonagall walk when she left the hotel?" I enquired.

"Away from it." I felt like burying my head in my hands at the stupidity of her answer. "Up towards all the shops."

Seeing as there were shops in both directions I was forced to point and indicate the direction I presumed Elsie might have headed, towards Northgate Street. I was correct, as Mrs Croft's nod showed.

"How long were you outside for Mrs Croft?"

"Not long. No more than ten minutes."

"Did you see anybody acting suspiciously during this time? Anyone lurking or heading towards the walls or even *on* the walls?" Mrs Croft thought and then quietly shook her head.

So far Mrs Croft had given me some decent evidence to mull over but I was still getting nowhere with her so I decided it was best to wrap things up.

"Just a few more questions Mrs Croft... Do you know where the nearest steps up to the wall are?"

"Oh... I'm not sure," Mrs Croft answered dumbfounded. "Are they over by that coliseum place?"

By 'coliseum place' I presume she meant the amphitheatre. Needless to say, it was not the correct answer.

"Finally, Mrs Croft, I'm sorry to ask this but I am sure you will understand the necessity of this question... Have you ever practiced archery?" Mrs Croft readily shook her head.

"She didn't do it," I said to Thomlinson as we walked down the corridor back towards the lifts. "The only motive I could see in her killing her husband would be so that she could marry someone else but this is just a little *too* extreme for that if you ask me. If she was really so desperate to be rid of him she would obtain a divorce, regardless of her reputation. She doesn't seem clever enough think of something as elaborate as using an urban myth to help herself get away with the crime either."

"Legal or not, we aren't letting this person get away with it. Murder is still murder and even if we can't get this killer on a direct charge we'll be able to get him on another… Hiding evidence… Not declaring his intentions… We'll get him for something, you mark my words Proctor."

I ignored most of Thomlinson's tirade against the urban myth and continued with my own thoughts.

"I'm concerned about that possible gap between Elsie leaving and coming back to the hotel. It would give her more than enough to time to take up position on the walls and shoot Croft before coming back down via the newsagents."

"You're forgetting one thing… Mrs Croft's statement that she walked towards the crossing. If it *were* MacGonagall that committed the crime she would have had to take a hell of a walk just to get into a shooting position, especially if she were headed for Northgate Street." I scratched my chin in thought and soon came up with a solution.

"What if she never got as far Northgate Street? What we learnt from Mrs Croft was that MacGonagall was headed *towards* Northgate Street. But that doesn't mean she went that far. She could have easily gone down St Werburgh Street and then slipped up the access ramp behind the cathedral."

"Still doesn't work though. I'd say that was a walk of at least three or four minutes. Too long to risk. It's enough time for Croft to come back early and re-enter the hotel."

"It *would* give opportunity to hide the weapon though. There are plenty of bushes down there. She could have hid the weapon under one and then collected it on the way to killing Croft."

"But how would she know to hide it there? She could have easily found out Croft was staying at the hotel by checking the guest list, but how would she know that he was going to be outside after midnight?"

"Perhaps that was a bonus," I guessed. "Perhaps it was just serendipitous luck… Or perhaps… Perhaps she was working with someone else… Perhaps they planned to lure him outside when she was in position… The porter perhaps? He left just after her according to Mrs Croft so it's possible… They could even be in a relationship for all we know!"

Thomlinson slapped me across the back for my good thinking and we headed downstairs and towards the 'Brasserie' restaurant where Cole Spencer, the porter, would be waiting to be interviewed.

He was again youngish, perhaps in his early thirties, with black hair and a shaven face so babyish that it begged to be covered by some hair just for the sake of making him look more mature. He was alone at a table in the centre of the room and nervously twiddling his thumbs. A classic sign of guilt if ever I saw one. Thomlinson and I sat opposite him and he looked up with a scared, puppy dog look in his eyes.

"Why did you leave the hotel between quarter past and twenty past midnight?" I asked him straight off the bat.

"I… I didn't," he stammered back. "I was at my post… You can ask Ir…Irving…"

"Irving?"

"Irving… He's one of the security guards. From Berlin. He'll back me up… I *never* left the hotel."

"If you never left the hotel then can you explain why Mirabel Croft claims she saw you leaving?"

"She's lying," Spencer yammered, becoming irritable.

"Either she is or you are. Which of you is it?" He was visibly flustered.

"It's her," he persisted. "She's a lying bitch. You can't believe a word she… she says…"

"And why is that? How do *you* know this?"

Sweat running down his brow. I sensed he was about to break, which would have been a world record had it actually happened.

Spencer didn't answer me. He looked down at his hands and moved his lips as though uttering a prayer.

He was guilty.

He had something to hide and he wasn't doing it very well.

"You know we're going to be looking at the CCTV cameras to see who left and who entered the hotel? Tell the truth and I might let you off with a slap on the wrists if it turns out you did anything bad." Spencer clammed up and refused to say anything. "As for shooting Dewi Croft... Well he was Welsh and within the walls. That's legal isn't it?"

"You should know. You're the policeman."

"It's only my job to investigate what people report as a crime. Not define it. The ones who've committed an actual offence get put away and the ones who haven't get a ticking off and told to stop bothering people. Think of me as a peacekeeper. Now tell... What were you doing leaving the hotel?"

"I... didn't," he persisted. "I didn't... I didn't..." This line of questioning was getting me nowhere.

"Tell me about you and Elsie MacGonagall. Are the two of you in a relationship?"

"NO!" Spencer sharpened determinably. "There was nothing going on between me and Elsie."

He seemed remarkably sure of himself. Almost as sure as Elsie had done when she claimed that she had left the hotel at twenty five past twelve.

"How do you mean *was*?" I picked up. "Does that mean there *wasn't* anything going on but now *is*? Is that why you went outside? For a brief rendezvous with Miss MacGonagall? For a tryst in the dark of the rows? A dirty fumble outside the *Edinburgh Woollen Mill*?"

Spencer began to grind his teeth and his nervousness was beginning to fray towards anger. A good sign that he would soon give me what I wanted to know.

"Where did the two of you go? There's a nice quiet spot behind St Peter's church…" Spencer's fingers twitched and I knew I might be onto something. I smiled. "So you and Elsie met up behind St Peter's church. Was it just to kiss or was it something more? Did you stick your greasy little fingers up her skirt and have a play? Did she wrap her claws around your tiny cock?"

"NO!" he shouted. "I *didn't* leave the hotel and there is

nothing going on between me and Elsie!"

"If you didn't leave the hotel and there's nothing going on then why are you being so defensive? An innocent man has nothing to be defensive about."

Spencer glared at me. He was definitely hiding something and to get it out of him I once again changed course.

"Explain what you were doing when you heard Miss MacGonagall screaming outside?"

"I was changing a light bulb in the lobby," he answered earnestly.

"Isn't that the caretaker's job?"

"The porter and the caretaker are the same person around here at night."

"So if I asked you to point out which light bulb it was you could answer me?"

"Yes."

He was growing more confident, becoming extremely sure of himself, so sure that he didn't expect my next question and was taken completely off guard.

"Which light bulb was it?"

Spencer's face flustered and his jaw opened and closed

whilst he tried desperately to pick a light bulb. There was no answer and he remained silent.

"You weren't changing a light bulb were you? What were you really doing?"

He growled and slammed his fist against the table, reverting back to anger. He really couldn't keep a check on his emotions this one.

"I was looking after the concierge desk for Wendy. She wasn't supposed to leave the desk until Elsie returned but I offered to take over for five minutes so that she could attend to one of the guests who wanted room service. We're not supposed to cover for each other but so long as the management never find out its fine." It sounded plausible but if this were the same Wendy I was thinking of then how could she have been outside to tend to Elsie if she was also tending to one of the guests?

"I'm presuming Wendy had finished tending to the guest as, according to Miss MacGonagall, she was the one who brought her back inside."

"She was half way up the stairs when the scream came. She dropped her tray and went running out." A likely story!

"Mr Croft was on the street, dead. I called the police and waited outside for them to arrive."

"Did you see anybody on the walls whilst you were outside? Anybody suspicious?"

"No."

"Did you see anybody else at all?"

"No."

"Ever practised archery?"

"No."

"Where are the nearest steps up to the wall?"

"Next to the hotel."

His last four answers came swiftly and they did me little good, with the sole exception of the last. As he knew of the steps next to the hotel he could have easily got up and down them and back into the hotel very quickly without anybody noticing. But that didn't explain how he would have been able to dispose of the weapon, nor where it was hidden before the murder.

Also, once again there came the issue of how he knew that Dewi Croft would go outside after midnight. That part didn't make sense, unless it had been a part of the plan for someone to lure him out of the hotel and the killer just got lucky. The CCTV, I hoped, would answer at least some of those questions.

They would certainly highlight the holes in Spencer's story. He had no alibi of which to speak and either he or Mirabel Croft were lying about him leaving the hotel.

I thought of something else concerning the disposal of the weapon.

How quickly could Spencer have disposed of it before returning to the hotel? The distance to the canal was about four hundred meters and the river was further, too far to get there and back quickly, so I again ruled that out. It would take the average man or woman, in good shape, which Spencer was, around three minutes to get to the canal and back at a run. Almost certainly, if he *had* been the one who shot Mr Croft, he would have been flustered when he came to MacGonagall's aid, something which she would have maybe noticed. Unless he had only disposed of the weapon afterwards or had somebody else do it for him. Could that accomplice have been Elsie MacGonagall? Perhaps. She could have gone onto the wall by the cathedral, waited for

Spencer, shot Mr Croft and then escaped with the weapon whilst he returned to the hotel as if nothing had happened.

It did seem an odd and convoluted way to do things. I wasn't convinced that this was the solution. The other option was that he left the weapon on the wall and after Elsie had discovered the body he then ran to the canal to dispose of it before calling the police...

But again that was a risky strategy. Somebody else could have called us in the meantime and the jig would have been up.

No solution I could think of made much sense.

"How fast can you run?" I asked.

This perked Spencer up and he answered freely without any nerves, as though he thought I were asking him casually.

"I won a few trophies when I was young... I was in the *Handbridge Sprint Team* in high school." He sounded especially keen to tell me this.

"And what about these days? Do you keep up with the sprinting?"

"Sometimes. I go to the gymn and occasionally I'll test

myself against my friends."

"So how fast are you? Are we talking Usain Bolt? Mo Farah? Ann Widdecombe?"

"I think somewhere between Ann Widdecombe and Mo Farah."

"Well that's fast. Ann Widdecombe can be quite the runner when she wants to be."

"Well let's just say that if Ann Widdecombe was chasing me I could outrun her."

Spencer said this with such confidence and panache that I almost forgot that he had been a gibbering wreck mere moments before. His confidence gave me the impression that he might be something of a lady's man, so I tried asking about relationships again, being more subtle this time. He didn't catch on.

"You single Cole? Seeing anyone? Anyone at all?"

"No. Can't say that I am."

"What was the name of the last woman you kissed? A handsome young fellow like yourself must get a few offers."

"I don't know what her name was. We just kissed, spent

the night together and then went our separate ways." He sounded as if he were avoiding the question by being vague. Most people don't sleep with someone without knowing their name. Was he trying to avoid the truth that the last person he kissed was Elsie MacGonagall?

"When *was* this? Can you tell me?" There was a long and revealing pause.

"Last week. Thursday," Spencer answered eventually.

I leaned back in the chair and thought over his evidence.

He had gone from nervous wreck to angry young man to supremely confident cad in the space of a few minutes and that suggested he was definitely hiding something. If he had nothing to hide why go through the first two emotions? An innocent man has no need to be nervous or angry. An innocent man, by virtue of the fact he has nothing to hide, will be free and easy and give you everything you could wish to know.

That wasn't Cole Spencer. Cole Spencer *wasn't* innocent. Certainly, how he *could* have killed Croft was still a puzzle to be solved but, if he were the killer, then it wouldn't be too hard to find a viable solution.

I stood up and made an indication to Thomlinson that I was done. Together we walked back into the lobby where I spied Elsie MacGonagall leaning against the concierge desk looking mournful and worn out.

"Have Spencer brought down to the station. He's hiding something and I want to sweat it out to him." Thomlinson gave a nod in return and retreated back into the restaurant whilst I casually ambled over to Miss MacGonagall.

"Are you alright Miss MacGonagall? Is there anything I can do to help?"

"No... I don't think so," Elsie replied sadly. "It's just... Seeing Mr Croft on the ground like that..." I put a hand on her shoulder.

"It's hideous, I know. But once you go home and get some sleep you'll feel much better. Do you have anybody who can pick you up? A boyfriend perhaps?" Elsie's eyes momentarily flickered towards the restaurant before she shook her head.

"I'm sorry to ask this Miss MacGonagall... But there is one more thing I really need to ask you before I go. When you discovered the body and Cole Spencer came from the hotel, did he look flustered at all? As though he had been running a great distance?" Miss MacGonagall looked incredibly confused.

"No... I don't think he did... If he was then I can't say that I noticed."

I headed up Eastgate until I reached the crossing, then turned up Northgate. The route from the Grosvenor to King Street seemed quite a distance and I began to think about how there was probably a cigarette merchant closer to the Grosvenor than the place Elsie had brought from. As I passed by the *Forum* shopping centre I took a brief detour towards the newsagents on the outside of the building. Looking at the opening hours in the window I was disappointed to find they closed at seven.

I moved on, looking down St Werburgh Street towards the cathedral, all lit up and greeny-grey in its unremarkable beauty, and tried to recall if there were any newsagents down that way. There were none that I could immediately think of but on my return, I decided, I would briefly investigate, just on the off chance.

I continued my way down Northgate and saw nowhere that sold cigarettes so late as midnight.

At last I came to the shop opposite King Street and was immediately curious. It was the only place that was still open, even the two pubs opposite had closed down for the night, and there was almost nobody about who might be considered passing trade. There were no students, no night clubbers and no, or at least very few, night shifters coming by in order to stock up on late night essentials. In short, apart from this one place, Chester city centre was as quiet and as sleepy as the proverbial tired sloth.

Inside I found a single girl of the bored and moody type with one hand on her cheek and the other resting against the counter. I picked out a few magazines from the topmost shelf and, along with a handful of chocolate bars, I took them to be paid for.

"You don't happen to know a friend of mine do you?" I asked pleasantly as my totals were being summed. "Elsie MacGonagall. She was in here earlier?"

"You want to get yourself some friends your own age you old fart!" I tried not to act offended, although I really was. Who wouldn't be when some young split calls them an old fart? Mind you, the top shelf magazines probably didn't help my reputation much. Still, she must have known who I meant as she knew MacGonagall was much younger than I am.

"I was only concerned about her is all. She was round my place earlier tonight and she was in quite a state. Did she look at all flustered or worried or in a hurry when she came in here?"

"What's it to you, you fucking old custard?"

OLD CUSTARD! That was a new one on me. I would have to use it sometime.

Didn't reply. Waited for my change to be rudely thrust towards me and left without saying a word. I would get nowhere in there and I already had all the information I wanted anyway.

Rather than head back down Northgate I decided that it was worth investigating the walls, forgetting that I had intended to take a nose down St Werburgh on the way back to Eastgate.

I ambled my way north, noting that the right hand side of the street was especially dark when compared to the left side. It didn't hamper my movements but I considered it would be perfect cover for any escaping assassin. Who would see anybody walking down from the walls and then along the left hand side of the road? Very few people I shouldn't have wondered, less if there was nobody around.

I came to the Northgate, nowhere near as grand as Eastgate but far more pleasing for its simplicity, and the first thing I noted was a security camera sitting atop a pole at the bottom of the steps. The footage would be of use to the investigation, I thought, as I passed underneath. If anybody had passed this way it was bound to have spotted them.

At the top of the walls, from the bookshop, there was an overhanging light showing the walkway ahead, which was mostly in darkness. That was the trouble with Chester's walls at night. Some parts, such as down by the race course, were well lit. Others like Newgate and the run up to it had only sparse lights here and were there just to keep the health and safety nutters happy.

The stretch running by the canal was another such part and the next light I could see was some thirty meters ahead, a long way in the dark. After walking for a short while I looked over the edge and saw nothing but the black chasm of the canal, the lights along the tow path being even sparser than those on the wall above. From what I could see the towpath was narrow and it wouldn't have taken an Olympian effort to casually toss something into the water. But given the drop I was certain that the weapon would have made a large splash. There was a chance that someone nearby *might* have heard it but the problem was that there were only a few houses nearby, all clustered on the bank opposite King Charles Tower, and most people walking these parts of town at that time of night, it has to be said, would have been too drunk or half asleep to notice such an insignificant thing as a splash in the canal.

I passed the King Charles Tower, an interesting beast to behold, and turned onto the stretch of wall that would take me back to Eastgate, the disposal route. It was well lit, or at least better lit than the stretch of wall by the canal, and I thought that any man or woman running down these parts could easily be seen by someone below. Then again, although this was the case, much of the wall was surrounded by trees to the left and there was nothing much except the 'Abbey Fields' on my right. There wouldn't be many people walking below at any rate.

Nevertheless, there were a few houses and it was possible that one of the residents had, by chance, seen something through a window. It would be luck if they had but it would be worth sending a couple of uniforms to find out.

Whilst I continued towards Eastgate I thought again about how the assassin could have escaped from the walls.

I had already cemented in my mind that he wouldn't have gone towards Newgate because of the darkness and dangers of the gate itself. It was also quite a task getting down to the river from there.

That meant the killer *had* to have escaped north towards the canal, where I presumed the weapon would have been disposed of. And then, I assumed, the killer would have wanted to get off the walls as soon as possible and that left only a few places to choose from.

The furthest point on this stretch was down by the railway and the water tower but that was quite some distance and almost all of it was lined with houses and apartments so the chance of being spotted up there was high.

After that was Northgate and, as we know, there *is* a security camera at the base of the steps. We could easily catch the killer if he had escaped by that route. He could have alternatively backtracked and escaped through Abbey Square *or* he could have gone the other way and escaped into the city through Kaleyards. That would have meant crossing the *Iceland* car park and there was sure to be CCTV there somewhere.

I was also sure there was a security camera in Abbey Square.

Wherever the killer had escaped from he would have been caught by a security camera somewhere along his route.

It would, therefore, be only a matter of checking all the footage to deduce which exit it was.

Thomlinson was pacing up and down under the clock tower when I arrived and a couple of SOCOs were scouring the floor, looking for signs of the killer. DNA.

"Find anything?" Thomlinson asked impatiently.

"I checked out the newsagents. Elsie MacGonagall *was* in there as the girl behind the desk acted like she knew her. There's plenty of security cameras up that way so if she *did* do it she will have been caught by one of them!" Thomlinson nodded his approval.

"Well I don't think our murderer could have gone up to Newgate. There's a little bit of light going up to it but the gate itself is completely dark. There *are* lights above the steps but they look as though they haven't worked for years. I don't think anyone who knew the city would risk it."

I agreed. The lack of a weapon in the vicinity of the gate indicated that the person *had* to know the city, even vaguely, and any fool could tell you that Newgate wasn't the easiest part of the wall to get over.

Thomlinson scratched his head and then began to shake it hysterically.

"Something here doesn't make sense Proctor. Spencer said he was a sprinter but could he really have shot Croft and disposed of the weapon before anybody noticed he was missing from the hotel? If he disposed of the weapon *after* the body had been found that's awfully risky. And where did the murder weapon come from? Where was it hidden before it was used? If the killer was someone from the hotel then they couldn't have hidden the weapon on the walls because anybody could have come along and found it. Somebody would have noticed if MacGonagall or Spencer came into work with a crossbow. I'm sure Dewi Croft would have noticed if his wife had packed one in her suitcase. That suggests to me that whoever did the deed *must* have been from *outside* the hotel… Which begs another question. How did they know Dewi Croft would be outside after midnight? Was it chance? No. Why would you wait on the walls with a loaded bow on the off chance you spotted a Welshman? And how would you know he was Welsh? Was it a late night business meeting where the intention was to have him killed all along? Not likely. If that was the case why not just shoot him when he left the hotel?"

"It had to be somebody he knew," I suggested. "Or at least somebody who knew he was Welsh. The whole urban legend thing about how it's legal to shoot a Welshman proves that. No sane person would risk targeting a random person on the off chance they got a lucky strike. The urban legend *also* proves it wasn't a random killing. The method is too specific to be random. Whoever this was knew what they were doing!"

"So who are we looking for?" Thomlinson put forwards. "We're looking for someone who knew Croft was Welsh *and* knows the area *and* somehow knew he would be outside the hotel after midnight. We're after someone who most likely went north to dispose of the weapon in the canal and who also probably escaped somewhere up that way too!"

We both leaned against the railings and looked at the spot where the body of Dewi Croft was being removed to an ambulance, both wondering what kind of deluded mind had dreamt up such a deed.

"This could be bad if handled the wrong way. There are

certain individuals in this city who will go off their rocker if they find out somebody has tried to test the old urban myth," Thomlinson claimed after a while. "Just imagine... If they *think* that one person has already gotten away with murder they'll think *they* can do the same. Then we'll have a job keeping them all in check. We'll have dead Welshmen all over the place. It'll be like King Harold all over again!"

Christ! King Harold! That had been several months which I would much rather forget. A few years ago some students had tried to claim that they were on the verge of finding King Harold's tomb, which another urban legend reckoned was located somewhere within the city. This had inevitably led to an influx of treasure hunters and would be Indiana Joneses prowling about with spades and trying to dig up every historical sight they could, which in Chester amounts to the entire city centre. This other urban legend was so ludicrous that I won't bother repeating it. You'll have to look it up yourself if you want to know what it is.

For myself and the rest of the city police it had been a complete nightmare. We were up to our ears trying to stop half the city from being destroyed by treasure hunters who were all seeking something that didn't exist. Sometimes I lie awake at night thinking about it and even today, at least once every couple of months, some fool will be brought into the station in order to be told that he is wasting his time looking for the man or his tomb.

"How can we *stop* it becoming like King Harold? Surely if we have the walls *and* Eastgate Street closed off people will know something is awry?"

"You're right. We can't keep it hidden. But there's no rule that says we *have* to release what we know straight away. All we have to say is that a man has been killed outside the Grosvenor and we are investigating."

"We'll have to release the information sooner or later though." I said. "We're going to have to say *how* he was killed and *who* he was. We may even have to appeal for information."

"Not if we work quickly and catch this killer. We know we're looking for someone who knew he was outside the hotel. Someone who knew he was Welsh. This wasn't a random attack. We're looking for someone who could have potentially drawn him out of the hotel if needed… We can trace this killer in a matter of hours if we try." Thomlinson turned to face me. "You've got until sunset to work out who did it Proctor... I'm arranging a press conference for just after so you'd better get a move on!"

Sunset.

That didn't give me a lot of time. And, to make it worse, there was nothing else I could do until the SOCOS had concluded their crime scene analysis and someone had gone through all the CCTV footage from the Grosvenor and around the city centre.

That would be breakfast time so I took the opportunity to drive home, to where I could collect my thoughts and work out how this murder was possible. Alas, everything that went through my mind had already passed through at least once before and as the Bee Gees rattled from the car stereo once more I despaired.

The whole thing, especially how the murderer had known Dewi Croft would be outside at the right time, seemed impossible.

Who knew he would be in Chester? Mirabel Croft?

No. I couldn't see her killing her husband. Not for the motive I had on her. If she was so desperate for a child then surely she *would* have divorced him. Unless she was already pregnant by somebody else and wanted him out of the way.

But again, why go to all the trouble of killing her husband when she could have just divorced him and got a huge chunk of his fortune to go with it? To get *all* of it? Most spousal murders aren't as calculated as this one was. They're committed in anger on the spur of the moment, usually with a knife or a nearby blunt object or a frozen leg of lamb. Most women don't lure their husbands to somewhere they can legally be shot with a bow and arrow.

No. This didn't seem like a spousal murder.

It was more likely to have been committed by someone like Cole Spencer or Elsie MacGonagall rather than Mirabel Croft.

That raised other questions about the whole timing of the murder, the disposal of the weapon, how they knew Dewi

Croft would leave the hotel after midnight. It was easy to surmise how they knew he would be staying at the hotel, they could have checked the booking reservations.

The whole murder made absolutely no sense when you really thought about it.

Clearly, I thought as I was reaching the edge of the city centre and coming into Boughton, there was something that I was missing.

On my salary I could buy myself a large, spacious, middle class home in Upton Park or Handbridge. A place with a large garden and a double garage and all sorts of rooms for relaxing and entertaining.

Instead I live in a two bedroomed, former council terrace in one of the city's more lower class areas. Some snobbish types might sneer at this, but it is by no means a bad place to live and it suits me well enough. I have no *need* to live anywhere else. There is only myself and Corwen and we have no need for anything larger or grander. Yes, it isn't what you'd call 'posh' or 'well to do' but the neighbours are a friendly bunch and we've never had any troubles. There are never any of the arguments or social competitiveness you get in middle class areas and where I live, not far from the main road into the city centre, (which makes getting to work *very* easy) we have ourselves a nice little community going on.

There are people who say that community is dead but I'd like to point them in my direction sometime. Prove them wrong.

Anyway, compared to the places where I had previously lived, (Old Swan, in Liverpool, and on the outskirts Newport,) this really was what you would call posh. Growing up in Liverpool I'd have called the people who lived in a house such as mine 'toffee bastards' and 'nobb scum.'

When I first married Anna we had decided to live in Pembrokeshire so that we could be close to her mother. However, as a serving police officer (I was just a uniformed plod in those days) the only work I could get was in either Newport or Cardiff. I had foolishly opted for Newport and for the next ten years I regretted that decision.

Newport, as most people who have been there will happily tell you, is the biggest shit hole on the planet. Even people *from* Newport will tell you how horrible it is. The only two other places that come close to being as bad as Newport are Silbury and Worton. The contender for the worst of the three is up for debate but Newport is definitely the worst when it comes to reported crime.

Hence, after the divorce and lumbered with taking care of Corwen all by myself, I opted to transfer to the tranquil, peaceful and mostly law abiding city of Chester. The worst crimes usually committed in these parts were the occasional burglary and drunkards urinating on historic buildings. Only once in a blue moon did anything truly serious come to the surface, this business with the murder of Dewi Croft for example.

All was quiet in the street when I arrived home, as it should have been, and when I listened I heard no loud and explicit noises rising from my abode. A good sign that Corwen and Beth had fallen asleep. I was smug that I had avoided hearing them for once and as I entered the hallway

I saw in the mirror that there was a smirk on my face.

I straightened it out as I took of my coat and shoes and entered the living room. Against the far wall behind the television, where there was an alcove between the window and the fireplace, we kept a bookcase that had filled with an assortment of random books collected throughout the years. Included amongst them were the textbooks from Corwen's three month career as a student of law.

Law is not the easiest of degrees to obtain. I should know for I myself studied law at Liverpool. If you're now wondering why it is that I'm a police officer and not a better paid solicitor or a barrister, it's because I found the thing so hard that I only just scraped a third by the skin of my teeth. Corwen, unfortunately for himself, had gotten good enough grades to enter one of the Oxbridge colleges, St Cyllin's, and from the start I knew that it could only lead to trouble.

The Oxbridge colleges work their students to the bone, every hour of every day, with no time for rest. Most universities work you hard. It stands to reason, but Oxbridge takes the biscuit when it comes to workload.

There is almost no time for a social life if you get my meaning. In the end, unless you become a tutor's pet, you must submit to life as an academic drudge or face the metaphorical guillotine.

Most people *do* manage to cope with the harsh workload and they come out of the other side of the grinder battered but generally alright.

The worst part is the snobbery. It seeps out of the walls like a slime and it oozes around you, sniffing you out and seeking any sign of weakness. Snobs and toffs gravitate towards Oxbridge and if you aren't one of *them* they will turn and sting you. They can turn on someone for having nothing more than a northern tint to their accent. The more broad your accent is the more likely they are to sting.

Spending the first five years of his life in Newport meant that Corwen had a deeply ingrained valleys accent which, even after sixteen years in Chester, had never diminished. And the snobs and the toffs had turned on him. They were merciless. Some even went so far as to beat him to a pulp whilst the masters, including the Vice Chancellor Lady Persephone Cambridge, looked on without doing anything to break up the fight. If you could even call it a fight. According to Corwen one of the masters had, at the end of it, come over and sneered about how he shouldn't have been so common. This, lumbered with the fact that he was doing a very hard degree at a very harsh college, meant that quickly came to a head.

After some public school jackalope had decided to throw him into the Isis Corwen broke. A police officer, Lewis, called me up at work, informed me of the situation, and then I had to drive the one hundred and fifty miles down to Oxford. I had never seen him so upset and even when we arrived home some three hours later he was still in floods of tears. Things had turned out fine in the end though. After deciding he would drop out Corwen was offered a well-paying job working for his cousins and he hadn't looked back since. I don't know what his job entails *exactly* but I do know the company deals somewhere in the area of 'international security.'

It is not my place to tell you any more.

We had retained the text books and it was to these I turned. I considered that perhaps there may have been a precedent for something like this happening, another 'legal murder' or a contradiction where an action was legal in one case but not in another. I spent an hour seated in my favourite armchair combing through all the sections on murder and manslaughter and checking the indexes for anything that concerned legal contradictions.

I found nothing.

Putting the law books aside I returned to the shelf and plucked out a thick city guidebook. Once reseated and rifling through the pages it didn't take me long to find something useful.

The law concerning Welshmen, it claimed, dated back to the time of Glyndwr rebellion when the future Henry V, Prince Hal as he was then known, was Earl of Chester. He ordered that all Welshman and Welsh sympathisers be expelled from the city and if caught after sunset they were to be decapitated. Finally, according to the guidebook, this law had never been repealed.

Well, I thought, that was something. There *was* a basis for the urban myth after all, supposedly. Welshman *had* been excluded from the city under pain of death in the past.

Supposedly.

Decapitation isn't the same thing as shooting someone in the back. It was possible therefore that our assassin could *still* be convicted depending on what the actual law said. If it existed. If the law mentioned killing Welshmen in general, without stating a specific method, then it might be hard to convict. However, if it specifically mentioned decapitation, dismemberment or any method that was not being shot with a bow and arrow or a crossbow then we would have him. It might be considered a minor niggle by some but it would be enough of a technicality to secure a conviction. That is, of course, if the guidebook was correct in its assumption that the law had never been repealed.

My next step, after scouring a few more guidebooks and coming up with similar information and often less, was to search the internet.

Here I found myself plunged into a strange world of nonsense trivia, urban legends and ridiculous laws that nobody in their right mind would ever even contemplate, let alone ratify. For instance, in California it is apparently illegal for a bumblebee to fly backwards. How, in any sane world, does that make sense? What damage does a backwards flying bee do and, more is the point, how do you enforce such a law? And who gets the blame? I highly doubt the LAPD have a special 'Bee Division' with their own bee jail where they house the habitual offenders.

I must have trawled through hundreds of such laws. Few of them making any sense. Laws such as those stating it's legal for a pregnant woman to urinate in a policeman's helmet. Again, in what world does that make sense? Why not just use the nearest public convenience? The only useful thing to come out of my internet trawl were a few similar 'legal murder' laws from around the world.

The urban legend about the Welshman wasn't just limited to Chester. Hereford had exactly the same law whilst York had a similar one that permitted the execution of Scotsmen. In Hong Kong it was said to be legal for a wife to strangle her cheating husband. Also, owing to the fact that on a ship the captain's word is law, murder is passable if the aforementioned captain allows it. The notion of legal murder was, it seemed, common.

At some point before dawn I concluded my search and

decided I would have a long soak under the shower. After the grizzly business of the crime scene, the questioning of the first suspects and the trawl through the world of ludicrous laws it actually felt good to let my mind rest and the water run over me. I lathered up with the soap and for a few minutes gloried in rubbing myself over, forgetting the world and all its horrors and just enjoying being alone in the cubicle. It's a strange phenomena but as I get older I find myself enjoying my showers more and more. This shower I enjoyed more than most.

As a child growing up in Old Swan I had dreaded Sunday afternoon bath times. Fifteen minutes spent sitting in a mangy blue Bakelite bathtub filled with tepid water and a rock hard, ancient bar of tar-soap that left an oily residue on the skin. Perhaps that explains why I now enjoy my showers more, because today they are far more luxurious than what I grew up with.

The shower I had that day was so enveloping and so relaxing that I had to physically tear myself away, forcing myself to shut off the water and wrap myself in the bath towel, following which I staggered towards the mirror.

For a man of fifty four I hold up well. There's still life behind my grey eyes, despite the fact I'm certain the crow's feet are getting wider and deeper as each day goes by. Then you have my hair, which I'm quite rightly proud of. Most men of my age have gone either bald or grey but I still have every one of my suave, chocolate locks. They *are* fading a little and that worries me a tad. Still, I can't complain. Thanks to my job I'm in a trim condition and even though I can't run as fast as I used to I can still give some of the whippers in uniform a good pasting when I need to. I also don't have any major health problems, unlike my dear old dad who suffered a string of ailments right from his mid-forties through to his early demise at fifty one. I had loved my dad and even though both Mum and I knew he hadn't long to live his death had come as a shock. I had outlived him at least and with that I consoled myself.

I shaved, a habit which I loathe but keep up because of my work, and dressed in a fresh shirt and tie before traversing back down the stairs to the kitchen where I found Corwen, alone, and fiddling with the radio.

"Alright Pops," he slid as I entered. Where he had come

up with calling me 'Pops' from I can't remember but I like the way he does it. It's different. "Didn't wake you up last night did I?" I shook my head.

"No. It was something else." I pretended to look around. "That girl you brought home still asleep?" Corwen shook his head, moving from the radio (which now danced to the strains of *Radio Deeside*) to the cupboard, looking for cereal.

"She went 'ome. Said she wanted to get in before her mam woke up. I offered to drive her but she said no."

I often wonder how Corwen manages to be so successful when it comes to picking up women, especially as he isn't exactly the best looking man in the city. You might say he looks a bit thuggish, what with his light brown buzz cut, single earring, scraggy goatee and the long array of tattoos up his left arm. His regular attire, as, predictably, he was wearing that day, consisted of a tank top, some battered jeans and an ancient trilby that I had been given by Anna's cousin. I had passed it onto Corwen after I had been promoted to CID and instructed not to wear the thing as it made me look like I was pretending to be in some noir thriller. He took good care of it, even managing to make sure it had survived the horrors of Oxford. I guess, as with any social interaction, Corwen's sexual success is all down to confidence. Being half Scouse and half Welsh he has a worrying amount of the stuff.

"Where did you go last night anyway?"

"Just up to the *Centurion* with Luke. Daisy was at that Phil Collins tribute concert down the racecourse. It was just the two of us. Oh, and speaking of mams…"

Corwen pointed to the kitchen table where the morning post was waiting. Our post arrived early- You can't always be sure of early delivery these days. On top of the usual pile of bills and magazine subscriptions there was a small postcard showing the Spanish steps in Roma. Without having to look much further I knew who it was from.

As I turned it over I beheld an overwhelming sense of dread. Anna and I, although we were divorced, were on friendly terms with each other but I still found any more than a few hours of her company nauseating.

We'd met in the eighties whilst me and some friends had been on a fishing trip to Cornwall. The first time I saw her she was sitting on a beach in a strapless swimsuit with a wide brimmed straw hat and dark sunglasses. She had instantly reminded me of Audrey Hepburn and that is exactly the reason why I scrambled down the cliffs in order to talk to her. Little did I realise that she took the whole Audrey Hepburn resemblance to absurd levels. She behaved, spoke and acted just like her most of the time. I still joke that our relationship was *'Breakfast at H. Samuels.'*

After a while even Audrey Hepburn can become irritating and having to put up with an increasingly fag hag imitation stretched my temper to breaking point.

We tried marriage counselling, or a single session, before deciding it was best that we went our separate ways, amicably settling that I would take care of Corwen in return for giving her most of our joint savings. In fact, the only three things I had left at the end of the marriage were our house in Newport, Corwen, and my job. To show how grateful I was for those I sold the house and transferred here to Chester.

We had remained in touch because of Corwen but that

meant, once a year and sometimes more, Anna would insist on flying in from Roma to see how 'her two favourite dahlings' were getting on. That would be what the postcard was about.

Darlings, Anna began. She always started her postcards with 'Darlings.' *It's been far too long.* By my reckoning it had been Christmas. Nine months. *I'm coming to England in a few weeks and would dearly love to catch up with you both. I'll be in touch to arrange things- Chow baby.*

That 'being in touch' would most likely be another postcard from whichever boutique country hotel she was staying in, arriving at the police station the day before she wanted to meet up. I sighed and threw the postcard back onto the pile.

"Where are we taking her out to this time?" Corwen asked. He was filling a bowl with cereal. I thought about it.

The last time she had been here we had taken her to the races and the time before that on a private gondola trip along the Dee, so this time around I supposed it had to be something simple like a meal at a fancy restaurant. I thought for a moment about one of the two restaurants at the Grosvenor. The Brasserie and one that had altered its name a few years back from the fairly decent sounding *Arkle* to the far more pretentious *Simon Radley at the Chester Grosvenor.* Whatever was wrong with *Arkle* I shall never know. In the end I hesitated, deciding, as I didn't have a particular fondness for the Grosvenor, to choose another restaurant.

As far as Anna was concerned it would have to be somewhere up market and not somewhere like *The Boot* or *Victoria*, both nice inns in themselves but not to Anna's taste.

"What about lunch at *The Commercial*?" Corwen suggested.

"Do the Commercial sell food?" If they did it would be the ideal place, seemingly upmarket and yet not pricey enough to break the bank.

"They're quite good actually… I took some bird there once." I looked up in surprise. Corwen didn't usually go on dates as such and it came as something of a shock to discover he might have actually been on one.

"Who was she?" I guttered, trying to retain my surprise

and still thinking it *had* been a date. Corwen shrugged.

"It was nothing major. Just some posh bird and her boyfriend who wanted us to arrange special security for their wedding." I squinted, wondering what sort of a wedding required security before the answer finally dawned on me.

"This wedding... It wasn't in Westminster Abbey by any chance was it?" I enquired.

"Aye. It was," Corwen replied bluntly, as though it were nothing. I sighed at my son's pretend stupidity and let the matter fall, moving to the rest of the day's post.

"Cheshire constabulary are this morning investigating the death of a man whose body was discovered outside the Grosvenor Hotel on Eastgate Street in suspicious circumstances, late last night. The man, who is believed to have been in his mid to late forties, was staying at the hotel when the incident occurred," the news reporter on the radio crackled before moving onto more mundane items.

Corwen stared at me, wide eyed.

"Shit! Who was it Pops?" There was no harm in telling Corwen. He would keep things to himself and not tell anybody.

"Dewi Croft... Media magnate from Wrecsam. Shot in the back with an arrow." Corwen appeared startled and I saw him frighten. No surprise since he was born in Newport and held a very long line of Welsh ancestry on his mother's side.

"Was it... You know... *That*?" It seemed everybody, including Corwen, had heard of this urban legend except me.

"Yeah. I reckon so. If it wasn't... *that*... then why go to all the trouble of shooting him inside the walls after midnight? It's too coincidental to be anything else."

"What if they just *wanted* you to think it was that? Or someone who wanted people to *think* it was that?"

"Who would *want* to do such a thing though? What purpose would it serve?" I scoffed. "Whatever the reason it was obviously their intention to shoot a Welshman, Mr Croft, inside the city walls after midnight."

"I thought it was after dark?"

"Dark... Midnight... It makes no difference. A man was killed."

"So what are you going to do? If this was a legal killing…"

"That's an important *if* Corwen. If it isn't legal we're all good and whoever did this will go down for a long time. If it is legal what happens will very much depend on what the law says about contradictions. Killing a Welshman might be legal but murder, which this is, of anybody, is still *illegal*."

"What about precedents? Anything like this happened before?" Corwen now seemed more intrigued than afraid. I shook my head.

"Not that I've found so far. This looks like it could be a first."

Corwen scratched at his scrappy facial hair and lifted his eyes to the ceiling.

"I could get Glenda to ask her dad. He's a solicitor I think." I approved. Glenda was one of the women whom Corwen worked with and if she hadn't been engaged to someone else I would have played matchmaker between them. There had to come a time, and soon, when Corwen stopped sleeping around and found himself a permanent girlfriend. I had already made up my mind that if by the time he was twenty six this hadn't happened I would register him on one of those internet dating sites and force his hand.

That may sound deceptive but it is a parent's duty to ensure that their children live sensible, happy lives. No exceptions.

"Whoever killed Mr Croft isn't going to get away with it. If it comes down to it we'll pin something on him even if we have to make it up," I grimaced, moving to look through the remainder of the post.

"Need any help with that?" Corwen winked, giving a sly hint about his line of work. I glared at him over a water bill.

Despite having his own motorcycle Corwen and I often drove into the city centre together. It was an economy thing and it was convenient because we didn't work far from each other. Corwen's office was a series of rooms on the top floor of Watergate, above *Beresford Adams*, and extremely spacious as there were only seven of them working there. I, meanwhile, worked not far away in the Town Hall police station.

Our station, although central, was not great. It was a cramped annex to the main building with forty of us all thrown together over a couple of floors. When you added in all the things that were required at police station; cells, interview rooms and the like, there was barely enough space left to work in. There was hardly any space for the few vehicles we had and parking was limited. To cap it all our station was so well hidden that few people even knew it was there.

The city centre police force had previously been located in an old sixties tower block, down by the river, on the corner of Nuns and Grosvenor Road, shared with the main headquarters of Cheshire constabulary and divisional HQ.

When the building had been demolished ten years ago divisional HQ had gone up to Blacon, which in all honesty is not the most useful place to house divisional HQ, especially if you need to be in the east or south of the city, and the city centre police had been stuck in the most inconvenient set of rooms that the council could find. The worst part about this is, when they had replaced the old building with a swanky, modern construction, rather than do the sensible thing and give the city centre police a purpose built section, they had given at least half of the building over to the *Abode Hotel,* most likely because they helped pay for the place, without any concessions to the police whatsoever.

It didn't help, also, that we were treated with extreme derision by our colleagues up at Blacon and called 'a quarrelsome quota of mavericks.' Even the main constabulary headquarters (now in the middle of nowhere) didn't show us much respect as, once again, they were considering relocating our station further up the road to where they happened to be building a medical super centre. Once again putting us wherever happens to be a convenient dumping ground rather than in a proper, purpose built police station.

Thinking about the *Abode Hotel* set my mind back to Anna. The Abode certainly had a restaurant and a nice one at that. The station had had its annual Christmas lunch there this year just gone. They served this marvellous poultry dish, guinea fowl I believe, and it came with a delicious spiced consommé and a selection of vegetables. The only trouble is, despite each individual dish being relatively cheap, they make you order a minimum three per person so not only does the price rack up but you end up five pounds heavier.

Some people like that. I don't. I prefer to go out the same weight as I came in. In the end I opined that *The Commercial* would be cheaper.

On the way to the station I thought some more about *why* the murder had taken place where it did.

It was obvious, really. The location was *very* convenient. You could see people coming from a long distance away, there was a quick and easy escape route and there were convenient places to dispose of the weapon nearby. In the dark, being seen on the walls was unlikely and there was the added bonus of being able to fire down upon the victim for an easier kill.

Anywhere else inside the city walls, say in St Peter's

Courtyard, would make escaping and avoiding detection more difficult. There were a multitude of CCTV cameras about to observe every movement and it would have been a simple task to identify anybody walking around the streets with a bow. It would also be much more difficult to dispose of the weapon, less easy to access the canal or the river.

Whoever the killer was they had tried to be clever. They had tried to best the law, firstly by committing the act in a way that was believed legal and secondly by doing it in a way that made escape easy and detection difficult.

The thing with murderers who try to be clever is that they always slip up somewhere along the line. They miss something or end up trying to be too clever for their own good and in the process they make their identity all too obvious. This murderer, I assumed, was the latter and that was all down to the method.

No doubt they had assumed shooting Mr Croft and getting away along the wall made them undetectable and they no doubt had a supreme confidence that we would never find out who they were, and even if we did they would still get away with it owing to the urban legend.

They were wrong.

I pulled up into my parking space, which I had previously arranged with kind permission of the library, and made my way into the station. Sasha was behind the reception desk that day and I gave her a cheery smile as I entered. She was a nice enough girl, only joined up six months before, one of those who wanted to make a real difference to people's lives only to end up behind a desk. I'd have felt sorry for her but there's no time to feel sorry for people in the modern world. Besides, we all have to do the tough jobs when we're young.

"Anything else come through on the Croft case?"

"Baskin and Reeves are almost done with the CCTV. Shouldn't be too long. There's also a note from Pearson on your desk."

I smiled, left Sasha to her business and pushed my way into the CID office. Baskin and Reeves, two of the smarter DCs, were huddled over a computer screen and intensely watching the footage of Northgate street from the previous night. I didn't bother to interrupt and went instead to my desk, neat and tidy with the sole exception of my computer and a photograph of Corwen playing with his cousins, Marco and Will, as a child. Curiously, I can't even remember that photo being taken although I know it *must* have been taken in Bristol, where his cousins lived as children, as the Cabot Tower is visible in the background.

Attached to the picture was a note reading: *32' steel tipped, fibreglass field arrow- OP*. Note from Pearson, the pathologist. I correctly presumed the brief message indicated the type of ammunition that had been used to kill Mr Croft. I switched on my computer and then stared at the incident wall that had been set up in my absence.

I really couldn't help thinking that something was missing. I looked continuously at the board, examining every detail.

In the middle was a photograph of Dewi Croft, a rotund, pleasant seeming man who looked as though he got more pleasure from business than fun. Beneath him were gruesome photographs of the crime scene, Croft lying in a pool of his own blood with the arrow protruding from his back. A photograph of the arrow itself and pictures of the place underneath the clock where the arrow had been fired.

Along the right hand side were pictures of the current three main suspects: Mirabel Croft, Elsie MacGonagall and Cole Spencer, along with their relationships to Mr Croft. Spread around the board were all the details we knew so far.

And yet, as I continued to stare, that nagging feeling that I was missing something again played on my mind.

My computer beeped to signal that it had loaded and I forcibly drew myself away from the incident board, hitting up the internet and cycling through my favourites list until I reached *Ebay.*

I made a specific search for the exact type of arrow used to kill Mr Croft and Ebay returned only thirty results to my computer. The top result was exactly what I was searching for, a set of fibreglass arrows that had the exact same fletchings. The rest of the results were of a similar type but then I considered that these results were perhaps too specific. I doubt even archery professionals type in '32' steel tipped, fibreglass field arrow' into Ebay whenever they need supplies. So I returned to the search bar and started again, this time typing in '*Archery Arrows.*' I was brought nearly eight thousand results, all different varieties of arrows ranging in price from a few pounds to nearly sixty.

The green fletched arrow of the type used to kill Mr Croft were amongst the cheapest. It was therefore plausible, because human beings are greedy creatures who like to spend money but at the same time keep as much of it as possible, that the green arrow had been chosen because of its price. It didn't tell me a lot but it made me lean towards to the idea that whoever the killer was they were not a professional archer. A pro would, in all likelihood, go for high quality arrows that were more expensive, more representative of their dedication to the sport. They also wouldn't use Ebay to buy their equipment.

When you are passionate about something you will spend all the money you can to ensure you are the best and to get the best quality equipment. In most cases you buy slightly more expensive equipment because it stands to reason that it will be better quality than the cheaper equipment. This suggested that I wasn't dealing with a professional but someone who was an amateur, someone for whom archery was more of a hobby than a way of life.

It may have been that the killer was no sort of archer at all. It may have been that they only bought their bow and arrow with the intention of killing Mr Croft.

Ebay is not the only place to get sports equipment. If you wanted something in a hurry, say if the killer had only planned the murder the previous morning, then a sports specialist had an advantage over the internet. The equipment would be there in the store and available to take away without the need to wait. I closed Ebay and in its place did a search for shops that sold sports equipment.

There were more in the local area than I realised, especially around the Sealand industrial estate where I discovered a hitherto unknown *Sports Direct* store. Then again it's not surprising I didn't know it was there as I don't go into that part of the city very often.

A lot of the shops up there were *too* specialised to be what I was looking for. Golf stores or fishing shops. None of them appeared to be specialist archery stores but there were a few that looked as though they might sell the relevant equipment. Sports Direct sells almost everything so I believed there was a chance that's where the arrow came from. A quick search of their website revealed, to my disappointment, that Sports Direct didn't sell *anything* to do with archery.

Still, there were plenty more places in the city that *might* sell them and I wrote a quick note to get Baskin and Reeves to check them out once they were done with the CCTV.

Then, as I stared at the map of Chester on my screen I realised what I had been missing.

Somehow, previously, it hadn't clicked with me but now it did click and in a big way. The killer had shot Mr Croft from the wall, that much was clear. But then if it were someone from the hotel they would have had to have passed Mr Croft's corpse on their return to the hotel. Even if they had taken one of the exits that did not come out onto Eastgate Street then they would have still had to have passed the body. Surely, if that were the case then the person involved would pretend they had discovered the body to help divert suspicion.

This pointed the finger at Elsie MacGonagall.

She could have exited the walls at Northgate, passed by the newsagents and then come back and pretended to have discovered the body. She also didn't seem to be any sort of archery practitioner so it stood to reason that she would opt for the inexpensive arrows. She'd go for the simplest and cheapest option. As for her motive and premeditation... Well that was more difficult to divulge. If she was guilty I could work it out given enough time.

Sadly, Baskin and Reeves were done with the CCTV and they came over to shoot down my theory about Elsie MacGonagall.

"Sarge... We've finished going through the CCTV," Baskin said sharply.

"And?"

"Mr Croft left the hotel just before midnight and headed out down Eastgate in the direction of Grosvenor Park. At twelve fifteen Both Elsie MacGonagall and Mirabel Croft left the hotel. Mirabel Croft goes somewhere out of the CCTV range but she goes back inside before Mr Croft returns and doesn't come back out again."

"And Elsie MacGonagall?"

"She heads up Eastgate and then turns onto Northgate and disappears for fifteen minutes." I sat bolt upright in my chair, thinking we had her. "It looks like she *was* having a dalliance with Cole Spencer. He leaves the hotel five minutes after she does, heads up to Northgate then vanishes for ten minutes. Our bet is they were having it off in some nook somewhere."

"When they reappear Spencer goes back to the hotel and MacGonagall heads right up Northgate street to the newsagents." My heart sank. The chances of the murderer being any of the three main suspects was vanishing before my eyes.

"Any sign of either of them going up the wall?"

"No Sarge... *But* Cole Spencer returned to the hotel only moments before Mr Croft was shot and by our reckoning he might have seen him coming. As soon as he gets into the hotel he makes a phone call. Could have been calling someone on the wall to tell them Croft was approaching." My heart made a leap.

"Through the hotel phone or using a mobile?"

"Looks like a mobile Sarge." There was a glimmer in Reeves' eye as he spoke.

We had him. We had the killer in our sights and within

only a few hours of the murder.

Alright, so we didn't know *who* he was but we had a potential accomplice and, as was usual practice, once we had the accomplice the murderer was never too far behind. And *because* Cole Spencer *was* an accomplice we now had a clearer idea of how the murder had played out.

Dewi Croft had left the hotel around midnight, flirting with Elsie MacGonagall along the way. Then Elsie MacGonagall had left the hotel, followed by Cole Spencer. After he had screwed with Elsie he returned to the hotel, moments before Croft. I speculated that Spencer had earlier contacted the assassin and informed them that Croft was ripe for the taking. The assassin had then collected his bow and arrow and hightailed it to the Eastgate clock where he waited in the shadows until Spencer gave the next signal. That signified to me that he *must* live somewhere nearby, somewhere close to the city centre. He *had* to also know Cole Spencer who, on his return to the hotel, had called to send the signal to the assassin that Croft was on his way. The assassin had then crept out of the shadows and fired.

Then he had ran, disposed of the weapon and got clean

away, thinking nobody would be any the wiser about what he had done. He and Spencer probably thought they had been so clever *and yet,* as is always the case, they hadn't outsmarted the police. Few ever can. This was all still supposition of course but it was, at the time, the most likely scenario.

I nabbed Spencer's mobile from his personal effects box and then moved myself into the interview room where he was waiting to be further questioned. I sat down and began tactfully, hoping he would confess on his own accord and make my life easier.

"So… Cole Spencer… Want to tell me what you were doing with Elsie MacGonagall?"

He leered at me.

"Don't you ever give up? I already told you…"

"Don't try denying it. CCTV shows you both heading up Northgate Street and then going in separate directions ten minutes later. Admit it… You were canoodling weren't you?"

"No."

"Ok… So if you weren't canoodling what were you doing?"

"We weren't doing anything because we weren't together," he denied.

"So you're telling me that the two of you were in the same stretch of Northgate and left at the same time *without* being together?"

"No. We weren't together."

"So who were you with?"

"No one."

"What were you doing? Spying on Elsie MacGonagall? Was she with a lover? Were you jealous?"

"No." I got the impression that Cole Spencer was a very petulant young man, especially from the way he kept snapping the word 'no' at me.

"Well you must have been doing something. What was it Mr Spencer? If it was legal then you have nothing to fear. We may be able to work something out." Spencer looked up at me, a sneer on his face. "Of course, there are other ways we could find out. We could sit here for the rest of the day until you tell us *or* we could just ask Elsie MacGonagall."

"She'll tell you as much as I have," Spencer lashed. "She'll tell you nothing. She'll keep her mouth shut to protect her precious job."

"Why would keeping her mouth shut mean she was protecting her job?" I enquired, knowing full well that he had just admitted that he and MacGonagall *were* together.

"Because staff relationships aren't permitted by the hotel management. They see them as a distraction." Spencer admitted, suddenly realising he had confessed his guilt. From that point on he ceased denying that he and MacGonagall were together. He knew there was no point in doing otherwise.

"Well, evidently they must be a distraction," I drawled sarcastically.

"Elsie and I didn't want the hotel finding out. They'd dismiss us if we did. And working together… We get these… urges!"

"Urges?"

"Sexual urges. We have to tame them otherwise we go out

of control." I cocked my eyebrow as he continued talking without shame. "Elsie and I. We had to get rid of the urges so we went up to the rows just outside *Animal* and she sucked my cock."

Outside Animal! It was appropriate, I gave them that much.

"That it? You didn't finger her, give her some cunnilingus in return?" Spencer looked at me as though I had just crawled out from the sewer.

"All she did was suck my cock. We didn't need to do anything else. We didn't have time."

"So you are in *love* with Miss MacGonagall, I presume?"

"Well why else would I let her suck my cock?"

"It's not unusual for people to just have sex for the sake of having sex with someone. Go into any nightclub in this city and you'll see people having one night stands all over the place." I was thinking of Corwen on that one. "There's even this thing 'called friends with benefits' these days."

"You mean fuck buddying? Or in your case I suppose it would be huck finning."

I leaned over. Hard look in my eyes.

"Don't get smart with me sunshine. I knew what huck finning was before you were even born and if you don't answer my questions truthfully I know a lovely chap called Thumper who's looking for a huckleberry friend to share his prison cell with. Now tell me straight. Is it the truth that you and Elsie and MacGonagall were in love and was the only reason she sucked your tiny cock outside *Animal* for sexual gratification and no other reason?" Spencer nodded, showing no fear. I'll admit, it was an improvement on when we first encountered one another but his lack of fear was creating a defiant attitude and that was only making things worse for himself.

"So after Miss MacGonagall gives you head you return to the hotel. Did you see anyone when you returned?"

"No."

"Are you sure Mr Spencer? Because less than a minute after you returned Mr Croft was shot in the back. You *must* have seen him coming up the street."

"I didn't. And if he was shot *a minute* after I can't have done it could I?"

He was getting cocky. The guilty always get cocky when

they think they've got one over on you.

"You couldn't have shot Mr Croft, no… But you could have helped arrange it. The only people who knew Mr Croft was out for a walk after midnight were in that hotel and *currently* I don't think *any* of you did it. So somebody must have told someone on the outside when he was coming. I think that someone was you, Mr Spencer."

"Prove it."

I put his phone onto the table.

"You were seen, in the intervening moments between re-entering the hotel and the death of Mr Croft, making a phone call. We again have CCTV footage to prove it. I think you were calling the killer to tell him Mr Croft was on his way. Is that the truth?"

Spencer remained silent. I pulled the phone back towards me and switched it on.

"All I have to do is check for phone calls made at half past midnight and we have both yourself and the killer nailed. We'll soon have the murder weapon because we're already dredging the canal and unless the killer wore gloves we'll have fingerprint evidence to go alongside what we already have. All I need is a name Spencer. Give it to me and you might get off lightly. A three year prison sentence with chance of parole at eighteen months instead of ten years without." Spencer once again remained silent. "All I have to do is check this phone!"

He remained silent.

I thumbed through to the recent calls list and hovered over the button, looking briefly at Spencer to see if he would capitulate. He didn't. He just gave a smarmy sneer and I soon found out why. He had tried to be a clever sod by deleting his call history.

"You know we can get back what you've deleted Mr Spencer? Nothing is gone forever. We have people up at Blacon who can tell us what was deleted and who you called and when… And we don't even need to use *them*… We can just call up the phone company and ask them who you called because every transmission that goes through the receiving station is logged. Your friend can't escape justice Spencer and neither can you. So tell me who it was and why he killed Mr Croft. You'll make life easier for everybody if you do." Spencer refused to budge or talk.

I had seen this many times before. People got caught in the act and they clammed up. Hoping that whatever they had done would just be forgotten about and go away. Childish.

You also won't be surprised to learn that it never works.

"I presume the name of your friend, the one who killed Mr Croft, will be in your address book?" I enquired, closing the empty calls list and switching over to the phonebook.

There was a whole host of names in the book, Elsie MacGonagall, his mother, Wendy who also worked at the hotel.

"You know we'll be checking through this phone book Mr Spencer. *Every* last person." Once again I tried to make a deal with him to confess but he failed to bite. "You could save us an awful lot of trouble, Mr Spencer, if you just tell us who killed Cole Spencer."

I waited for a response and when none came I stood up.

"Cole Spencer," I began. "I am formally arresting you as an accomplice to the murder of Dewi Croft. Anything you say will be taken down as evidence but you still have the right to remain silent."

On the way to his cell Cole Spencer cried.

I had no sympathy for him. He had tried to hide his part in the whole thing but he had failed, as those who try such things often do.

Now I only had the unenviable task of finding the killer. I now knew it was *definitely* someone who *wasn't* at the Grosvenor the night before.

It wouldn't take long for the lab at Blacon to extract the information from Spencer's mobile so in the meantime I decided I would retrace Dewi Croft's final movements. Mrs Croft had said that he had toured the *Deva Gazette,* so that was where I would begin.

The Gazette was not exactly the best newspaper in the city. It was quite fairly derided as a rag of tabloid trash, scandal and gossip, which is not surprising considering that their owners were *DAILY PRESS ASSOCIATES LTD*. It's one of those local newspapers that gets pushed through the door once a week and contains enough adverts to make your head explode. I never read it and always place it in the recycling bin straight off. If it were forty years ago I'd use it for toilet paper but these days I've been too pampered by quilted *Andrex* to do that sort of thing.

Their offices were located on Nicholas Street Mews in a splendid Dickensian building that had railed steps leading up from the street and an old fashioned lamp hanging over the door.

I walked the half kilometre from the station, there was no point in taking the car for that distance, and trotted up the steps.

The main reception was a little room off to the side of a short corridor. The receptionist behind the desk was of the flouncy, middle aged sort. The sort with rounded spectacles and a look that says they aren't happy with their lot in life. She glared at me with pitiable despair as I approached and held my badge out.

"D.S Simon Proctor… Is there a chance I could speak to your editor?" The lady nodded and reached for her phone. She dialled and I waited, listening to the dial tone on the other end of the line, which I presumed was internal. I could hear the other end without dificulty.

After a few seconds there was a disgruntled 'Yes?' from the other end of the line.

"There's a gentleman here to see you Mr Guinness. He says he's with the police."

"With the police? Is he important? Who *is* he?"

"He says his name is D.S Proctor... Simon Proctor." There was a loud, verbal grousing from the editor, Mr Guinness.

"I'll be down momentarily." The receptionist reiterated this to me and I gave her my best smile.

"You wouldn't mind if I asked you a few questions whilst I waited would you?" The receptionist preened herself as though I were about to ask her out on a date.

"Go ahead. I don't mind."

"Dewi Croft. I believe he was here yesterday?" The receptionist brightened considerably at the mention of his name.

"Oooh yes... Such a lovely man. He came round to all the staff and he spoke to us and he was very friendly."

"How many people work here?"

"Including myself and Mr Guinness, seven." Not too hard to be friendly to them all then.

"I understand he was thinking of buying out the newspaper? What did you think of that?"

"I thought it quite marvellous. It's about time someone took control of this place and got it back on track."

"Did everyone feel the same way?"

"No. There were a couple who weren't best pleased about it but…"

"Could you tell me who they were?" The receptionist shook her head and put a hand across her mouth.

"Oh no. I couldn't possibly. It would be like gossip mongering and my old mother would never allow such a thing."

Her old mother be damned, I thought.

"Please, it's important." The receptionist flustered, twisting her palms and sweating over the repercussions. I almost threatened her with wasting police time but thankfully it never came to that as she opened up.

"It was Rhyddian Barnard and Francesca Chalmers. They were up in arms about the whole thing. Mr Guinness wasn't best pleased about it either."

"Are Rhyddian Barnard and Francesca Chalmers here today?"

"Yes. They work desks opposite each other. Mr Guinness will be able to point them out to you when he takes you upstairs."

She began to shuffle about in her seat and twiddled her thumbs, as if she felt she had betrayed her colleagues.

"Why weren't they pleased about it? Mr Guinness too if you know the reason." I tried to sound as polite as possible.

"Well. Francesca works the gossip and agony aunt column and she probably felt that her job was threatened. Mr Croft was planning to the take the newspaper in a more upmarket direction and he was probably going to make her redundant."

An upmarket direction for the Gazette, eh? Not a bad thing in my opinion.

"And what of Mr Barnard? Why did he not like Mr Croft's takeover?" The receptionist looked around snakily and beckoned me closer.

"Well… I'm not one to gossip." She obviously was. "But

the chief reporter, Miss Lame, told me she saw them together in that Italian place down near the cathedral. From what she was saying they looked quite intimate."

"How intimate?"

"Candles. A single plate of spaghetti between them. An inevitable lip locking. A little bit *Lady and The Tramp* if you get my drift." I have never seen Lady and the Tramp so I couldn't comment on that particular reference.

"The last time I checked it wasn't a crime to fall in love."

The receptionist hurled an insulting glare at me over the top of her spectacles.

"No. But it's immoral when you have a *girlfriend*."

"So in your opinion, maam, Rhyddian Barnard hated Mr Croft taking over the paper because the woman he is having it off with might have lost her job?"

"That's about the short of it, yes."

"And what does Mr Barnard do for the paper?"

"He writes some sports articles and he does a monthly section on local folklore." My ears pricked up.

"What sort of things does Mr Barnard cover in this folklore column?"

"Oooh… All sorts. You have no idea how many ancient secrets this city holds. Rhyddian was telling me the other day about this thing called 'void theory.' The older and larger a place becomes the more likely things are to become buried and forgotten… Buildings, tunnels, vaults… They just get lost. It makes sense when you think about it. All you have to do is go down the side of the Forum Shopping centre and look at that treasure pit. Then there was that business with King Harold a few years ago…"

Oh God… Not King Harold again!

I was rescued from any more mention of him by the arrival of the editor, Mr Guinness.

Guinness was one of those managerial types, the kind who still exemplified the long dead callousness and selfish attitude of the yuppie. He was a tall man, approaching retirement, and looked as if he threw money at himself on a regular basis. His nose was hooked and he glared at me through piggy, soulless eyes. He held his hand out as he approached.

"Simon Proctor I presume? Mr Guinness. Editor in chief." His voice was booming and like that of a Victorian entrepreneur. "Come up to my office, we can talk in private. I presume this *is* a private matter?"

"The matter is a delicate one."

"Ah, I see," Mr Guinness ruffled.

He led me up a flight of steep stairs and through a door into a large newsroom. In the middle there was a conference table and in the far corner a set of desks with computers where the 'journalists' were busy working. They looked up with curiosity as we entered but then returned to their work. Guinness showed me to the side of the newsroom where there were two offices separated by a glass wall, the kind you used to only find in the *Bradford and Bingley* but now seem to crop up everywhere.

"So tell me, D.S Proctor," Guinness began, closing the door to his office and beckoning me to be seated behind this desk, "to what pleasure do I owe this visit from Chester's finest?"

"Dewi Croft," I said. "At around half twelve last night he was shot from the city wall underneath the Eastgate clock." Mr Guinness looked scared all of a sudden. "He was killed in the manner suggested by an old urban legend. I'm sure you know the one." Mr Guinness nodded slowly, a look of horror etching itself onto his face. "I understand that Mr Croft was here yesterday?"

Guinness nodded again.

"Yes. He was thinking about buying the paper from the *Daily Press*."

"And how did you feel about this?"

"Concerned," Mr Guinness admitted. "He was going to take the newspaper 'in a different direction,' so to speak. He was going to make it 'less tabloid.'"

"And you didn't think that this was a good thing?"

"No. I don't think it was a good idea. For a start such a radical shift would alienate most of our readers."

Readers? What readers? Nobody reads the Deva Gazette. It goes straight into the recycling bin or gets used as toilet paper by hard up students. "Our readers like what we have. They like the fashion tips and the gossip and the scandal. We're a good paper as we are. We don't need taking up market."

"Yes. I'm sure you don't," I responded sarcastically. "Did you voice your feelings to Mr Croft?"

"No. I didn't. If he was buying the paper and I argued against his plans then he'd be even more likely to fire me."

"How safe did you feel your job was considering he wanted to take the paper in a new direction?"

"I'm a part of the old guard and used to doing things in my own way. Croft would have certainly wanted his own man to come in and help shake things up."

"And what about the reporters? Would they have kept their jobs?"

"Mr Croft did confide in me that he was thinking about replacing Rhyddian Barnard or Francesca Chalmers. Perhaps even both."

"And why is that Mr Guinness?"

I folded my hands underneath my chin, intrigued.

"Once again, Mr Proctor, it has much to do with the direction in which Mr Croft was hoping to take the newspaper. Miss Chalmers and Mr Barnard are two of our more… populist journalists. What they write is not the sort of upmarket material that Mr Croft intended for the paper."

"Can I see some of their articles?"

Mr Guinness came back holding two black folders and

handed them over the desk as he sat back down. Each contained proof copies of the articles I had requested, one folder for Rhyddian Barnard and one for Francesca Chalmers.

I leafed through the folder for Francesca Chalmers whilst Guinness watched me. Her main news articles were scathing and showed she was not as unbiased in her writing as a good journalist ought to be. It was more opinion than journalism. There was one piece concerning plans to close the city cinema and build an ASDA in its place. Miss Chalmers spent most of the article talking about how terrible *she* thought the cinema was, how *she* never used it and how all modern films were just violent CGI filled rubbish. (This isn't so. I went to see *AVENGERS ASSEMBLE* with Corwen and his friend Luke and, despite my initial disappointment that it wasn't John Steed and Emma Peel, I enjoyed it.)

Her fashion articles, however, were worse than her general ones. She had no taste and most of the things she promoted were ugly, outdated things that can only be described as throwbacks towards the unfashionable end of the seventies. It was the sort of overpriced tat from fucking *Matalan* your grandmother always thinks you'll look nice in.

"Is Miss Chalmers a good worker?" I asked, doing my best to hide what I really thought of her work and continuing to go through the folder of proofs, stopping occasionally to examine an article.

"Oh she's *very* good. As you can probably see from what she writes she's a top class journalist. Much too good for a paper such as this."

"If she's such a top class journalist why hasn't she been poached by someone like the Chronicle or Fleet Street?"

"I honestly don't know," he answered. I knew... It was because he was incredibly wrong about the woman.

I moved onto the folder Barnard's proofs and it was immediately clear he was a far superior journalist to Chalmers. He had at least a little bit of skill and was deserving of a better position than working for the Gazette.

The first article was about a 2-0 drubbing for Chester F.C by Wrecsam in the cross border derby and it went into great detail about tactics and strategy and praising the performance of each side whilst offering select critiques and ideas on improvement.

Barnard's other sports articles, which covered everything from swimming galas to rugby matches and even a pool tournament, were equally well written and they showed that Barnard had an expert knowledge of sports. I guessed that he probably played a few as well.

In between the sports articles were the pieces on Chester's history, urban legends and folklore. There were some about excavations, like don at the amphitheatre and others assessing potential damage to the rows by late night revellers relieving themselves. Some just detailed history, like the story of Edward Langtry (husband of Lillie) who was buried in Overleigh cemetery or that blasted myth about King Harold.

Others took a more philosophical approach. One piece, dated a few summers back, concerned several theories about what might happen if a Welshman were to be shot after midnight. After wrangling with the possibilities, including an odd suggestion that the killer might be both acquitted and convicted, something which would be far too confusing for any jury to comprehend, Barnard came to the conclusion that anyone who successfully attempted to test the law would be acquitted but the law would subsequently be amended so that nothing of the sort could ever happen again.

I disagreed with his conclusion of course. Whoever *did* kill Dewi Croft was going directly to jail. Thomlinson and I were going to make sure of that, even if we had to personally lock them up in our own personal dungeons'.

It was still an intriguing piece though. It fingered Rhyddian Barnard as a highly creditable suspect. He had even mused over what would happen if someone ever decided to test it. Could he, I wondered, have taken it a step further? Tried to prove his theories?

I closed the folder and handed it back to Mr Guinness.

"I have to ask you a few questions Mr Guinness, as a matter of routine you'll understand. Can I ask what you did last night? Where did you go?"

Mr Guinness grumbled before he spoke.

"I stayed at home and watched television with a Glenfiddich."

"And what did you watch if I may be so bold as to ask?"

"An old film. It was that one with the nuns in a remote Tibetan monastery and they all go mad and jump off a cliff at the end." I vaguely remembered having seen something similar.

"Do you know what this film was called?"

"Erm. No. Sorry. I think it had Deborah Meaden in it." I'm certain Deborah Meaden is the blonde lady from that business programme but I didn't bother to make a correction. It wouldn't be that hard to search last night's schedules for a film involving mad nuns and find out if he was telling the truth.

"Do you have a wife or children or anyone who can confirm your alibi for last night?"

"No. No wife or child. I divorced a few years ago."

"Did you call anybody? Did you speak to anybody last night?"

"No. I didn't."

"Have you ever practised archery?"

"Yes. Well, not practised as such. I had a go during a team building weekend a few years ago but I wasn't very good. I missed the target every time."

"As a matter of course, who on that weekend was good at the archery?"

"Ben Jarmin… But he's no longer with us."

"Where is he?"

"Cardiff. Working for another paper. He was fired after a series of arguments over the way I run things here. He came in mouthing off once too often. So I fired him."

"And what about the people who still work here? What about the receptionist downstairs?" Guinness laughed at my suggestion.

"Julie? No. She was worse than I was."

"What about Rhyddian Barnard or Francesca Chalmers were they any good?" The eyes of Mr Guinness narrowed shiftily before he answered.

"No. They weren't very good." I got the feeling he was lying about at least one of them.

"But they did have a go?"

"Yes."

I looked Mr Guinness squarely in the eyes.

"Rest assured Mr Guinness, if you're lying about their

archery ability I will find out and I'll have you up before a judge. Now tell me the truth. Did either Rhyddian Barnard or Frances Chalmers have any archery skill?" Guinness looked at me, stone faced.

"No," he responded. He was lying. I *knew* he was lying. His eyes were shifting from side to side and one of the veins above his right eye was pulsating, an unusual side effect of lying which only occurs in a small minority of the population.

"Mr Guinness... This is a serious matter. Now please tell me the truth. Were either Rhyddian Barnard or Francesca Chalmers any good at archery?" I put on my hardest, most intimidating glare.

"No. They *weren't*," Guinness lied again. I folded my arms and waited in silence for him to tell me the truth. Guinness stared at me, his eyes narrowing and his lip curling with detestation.

"Perhaps I could speak to them both whilst I'm here. It'll save me dragging them down to the station for questioning."

"Why do you want to question them? My staff are

innocent. *They* won't have killed Dewi Croft."

"If *they* didn't do it then that means *you* must have done it," I sneered. Mr Guinness's face collapsed and he began waving his arms.

"No… No," he flustered. "I didn't mean it like that. What I meant was that they aren't the sorts to go around killing people. I wouldn't hire anybody like that."

"Sometimes people don't *plan* to become a murderer Mr Guinness. Even the nicest of men can turn nasty. Brian Victoria in Silbury last year…"

"Killed his wife didn't he?"

"Indeed he did. And all his neighbours said he was the mildest, meekest man who ever lived. He wouldn't have hurt a fly. One day he just snapped and stabbed his wife with a corkscrew. What I mean, Mr Guinness, is that you can't be sure that either Mr Barnard or Miss Chalmers didn't snap and decide to kill Mr Croft."

Guinness nodded at me in understanding, worried, before leaving the room to fetch the two journalists.

Moments later an attractive young man in his late twenties boldly entered the room. He had these short golden locks and shimmering, bright green eyes that had a playful seriousness to them. He held out a hand towards me and I shook it as he sat down in Guinness's chair. He looked comfortable there, with a future editor's air.

"Good Morning sir. Rhyddian Barnard," he announced proudly. I nodded the acceptance of his polity.

"D.S Simon Proctor. I need to ask you a few questions Mr Barnard. Is that ok with you?" Rhyddian Barnard gave a big smile.

"Fire away."

"First of all I'd like to ask you about your movements last night."

I thought it best not to mention Dewi Croft at this early stage, especially as I already had Barnard in my mind's eye as a potential suspect. He might, if I was lucky, slip and reveal something he shouldn't have known.

Barnard answered my question willingly and with a friendly smile.

"I was over at my girlfriend's house. All night. We ate, watched a film and then we went to bed."

"What film did you watch?"

"*The Black Cauldron.*"

"Was that on television or DVD?" If it was on television we could always check. DVD was not so easy.

"It was through *Netflix*." Ok, so it wasn't television but Barnard's Netflix account would show if he was telling the truth or not.

"And this was with your girlfriend? Can I ask her name? Just for the sake of checking the facts you'll understand." Barnard smiled and once again answered willingly.

"Her name is Carla Naismith. She lives on Duke Street, near the river. Just a few doors down from *The Cross Keys Pub.*"

He seemed expressly keen to tell me this, as if he was hoping to deflect my suspicions by being honest. However, despite the fact that it's generally better to be open with the police you can still be *too* honest.

"You say you went to bed after watching the film. What time was this?" Barnard blushed.

"It was a quarter to ten."

"A little early don't you think?" Barnard went red, as if he was embarrassed. I almost laughed at him but decided that I would make him feel more at ease instead. "If you and your girlfriend were having sex it's nothing to be ashamed about. Sex is a part of life. Is that what you were doing?" Barnard nodded. "How long have you and Carla been together, if it's not an impertinent question?"

"Ten years next Thursday."

"And you don't live together?"

"No. We've never got around to it."

Never got around to it? Good grief... Most couples move in together after only a year or two and yet Barnard and his girlfriend had been together for *ten* years and hadn't done anything like. Clearly he hadn't proposed marriage either as if he had he would refer to as his fiancée and not his girlfriend. And surely after ten years a proposal was long overdue. Most couples move forwards with their relationship quite quickly. After a year or so they move in together. Another few years after they get engaged, then married (of course) and then have kids if they want them. Usually this has all happened within the first ten years of their relationship. But this pair appeared to have well and truly stagnated. I began to probe further.

"Are you serious about your relationship Mr Barnard?" Rhyddian Barnard looked shocked.

"Yes. Of course I am. Why wouldn't I be? We've been together for ten years."

"But you don't live together? As you said yourself you hadn't got around to it. Most couples *would* have got around to it one way or another by now. And as you call her your girlfriend I'm guessing the two of you aren't engaged? You'd be married and possibly have a child by now if you were serious about the relationship."

"*I* don't want to get married." Note that he used the word 'I.' He didn't say *we* which suggested to me that his other half was hoping for something more from their relationship. I had a sneaking suspicion she wasn't ever going to get what she wanted, not from Barnard at least.

"Where did you meet Carla?" I was going off track, I felt, and needed to rein myself back into line.

"We met at the university."

"Chester?"

"Yes. It was at an AU night. I was on the rowing team and she did archery." ARCHERY! *Helloooooo!* "We got chatting and we became friends and… Well, you know how it goes."

Yes. I know exactly how it goes. Ten years later you find yourself in exactly the same place!

"I looked at some of your articles Mr Barnard. Was it Carla who gave you the idea for that article about the old urban legend? The one about shooting someone with an arrow?" I saw Barnard flinch. Then he smiled again.

"Yes. It was. Quite an interesting subject I'm sure you'll agree." I nodded at him, not letting slip for a moment that this was how Dewi Croft had been killed.

"Have you ever practised archery yourself Mr Barnard?"

"The last time I did archery was on a team building weekend a few years ago. Before that I did a little with Carla at university. I was no Robin Hood though."

"But could you at least hit the target?"

"Nine times out of ten. It's not too difficult once you grasp the basics. Right stance. Right way to draw. Get your ideal draw weight. I'm not very good though." I got the impression he was downplaying.

"I believe a Mr Dewi Croft visited this office yesterday. Is that correct?" I decided it was time to bring the subject around to the murder.

"Yes. Although I'm not happy about it." Again, he was being rather *too* open. "I get the feeling that he's going to make me redundant."

"Do you know why Dewi Croft wanted to replace you?" I inadvertently used the wrong tense and Barnard squinted at me.

"I don't really know. He said he liked my sports articles but he wasn't too keen on the folklore stuff. He said it was the sort of thing that belongs in a second rate magazine and not a serious newspaper." His lip twitched with displeasure.

"And that upsets you?"

"Damn right it upsets me. I've put a lot of time and effort into those articles. I know more about this city than anybody else. Take the sewers. Did you know that underneath Watergate in one of the old Roman sewers there's an early Christian church?"

"No. I didn't know that." It was an interesting fact, I gave him that much. "Would there be any chance of Mr Croft keeping you on for the sport? Your sports articles are as good as the folklore ones."

"I think he wanted rid of me because I'm part of the old guard." I noted that, as I had done, he had used the past tense. An interesting sign, but nothing conclusive. "I'm an example of the way he thinks the paper *shouldn't* be run. He made no secret of what he thought whilst he was here. We all knew he was going to bring his own man in as editor and that he was going to replace all the staff he didn't like."

"Yourself and Miss Chalmers?"

"Yes. Maybe one or two others as well."

"Did Mr Croft *tell you* he was going to have you replaced?"

"Not in so many words but when we told him what we did... The look of disgust on his face was... And when he announced he was 'taking the paper upmarket' and that 'things were going to change' Francesca and I knew that we were both for the proverbial."

"What did you do about this?"

"What any sane people would do. We both came in here to Mr Guinness and demanded he safeguard our jobs," Barnard said with the air of the pariah.

"And did he?"

Barnard laughed.

"No. Of course he didn't. He couldn't guarantee anything because he was going to be losing his job himself."

"What is your opinions of Mr Guinness? Is he a good employer?"

"Yes. Certainly. We all get bonuses for our birthdays. He treats us with respect."

"So say somebody came in here and started complaining about the way Mr Guinness runs things You would defend him I presume?"

"Yes. Definitely."

"What about when Ben Jarmin was fired? Were you here that day? Did you defend Mr Guinness then?"

"It was me who escorted Jarmin from the building. He refused to leave."

"What exactly was his argument with Mr Guinness?"

"He was constantly being told to simplify his articles, make them less elaborate. He used complicated language that nobody could understand and everything he wrote was always far over the acceptable word limit."

"The acceptable word limit being?"

"four hundred words for regular articles. One thousand for features." That sounded a little low and I sympathised with Ben Jarmin's position.

"What did you personally think of Mr Jarmin?" I questioned.

"Odious little shit who was always up himself," Barnard sniffed. "He always thought he was so good at everything and he wasn't afraid to let everybody know it."

"What about on the team building weekend a few years ago. Was he very competitive then?"

"It wasn't really a team building weekend... More an excuse by Mr Guinness to take a cheap holiday."

"Answer the question Mr Barnard!"

"Yes. He was very competitive, especially during things like the rock climbing."

"Were you glad when he was fired?"

"Yes." He paused a second and gave me a scowl. "Is this going to take much longer? It's just I have a deadline to meet!"

"One final question. Do you know anybody by the name

of Cole Spencer? He works as a porter at the Grosvenor."

"No. I don't know anybody by that name," Barnard answered. He was far too cagey in the way he responded and I knew in an instant that he was lying.

Rather than pull him up on his lie I simply bid him good day and awaited the arrival of my next interviewee.

Never in my career as a police officer have I come across as hideous a specimen. Not even Mirabel Croft came close to matching Francesca Chalmers for grotesquerie. Her face was trowelled with unsuitable makeup and she wore earrings that were so big you could have used them to play basketball. Brunette hair combed back with a Croydon face lift. Steretypical chav. You get the picture.

"What were you doing last night Miss Chalmers?" I got straight to the point.

Chalmers shrugged.

"I was washing my hair weren't I?" Her voice and lack of grammar shot straight through me.

"And did that take all night?" I asked, trying to sound as facetious as possible.

"Of course it does. A girl has to take her time over such

things. You don't then you end up looking like that flump downstairs." To me the receptionist hadn't appeared to have had bad hair but I was secretly pleased by what Chalmers said. The antipathy of the statement opened a secret door of enquiry which I could sneak down.

"Why do you call her a flump, Miss Chalmers? She seemed respectable to me." Francesca Chalmers laughed.

"She's one of them types. She's perfectly nice to your face but she'll start bitching about you the moment your arse is turned."

"So you don't get along?"

"Oh, I can get along when I have to. She's a bitch is all."

"What about your other colleagues? How do you get on with them? What about Mr Guinness? What about *Rhyddian Barnard*?" Francesca Chalmers rounded on me as though I had said something offensive.

"What's that old cow in the reception been spreading? She been telling you him and me been having it off has she?"

"No. Nothing of the sort," I lied. "But for the record, can I ask why she *would* say such a thing?"

"She reckons she saw us having some candlelit dinner in a restaurant but she didn't."

"Because, I am presuming, you have never had a candlelit dinner together?"

"Oh no... We have... It just weren't a romantic candlelit dinner." This left me confused. If it wasn't a romantic candlelit dinner then what sort was it? Were there any other kind of candlelit dinners? Maybe a century ago, but surely not in the modern era. Francesca Chalmers answered my questions before I had even asked them. "He took me out to dinner because my grandmammy had died and he was being a good friend." It sounded rubbish. Who has an intimate candlelit dinner after someone's grandma dies? Nobody, to my knowledge.

"So his girlfriend knew about the dinner?"

"Yes. She did." I made a mental note to check up on that piece of information later.

"Out of curiosity, what *do* you think of Mr Barnard? Do you find him attractive? If he asked you out on a date what would you say?"

Chalmers blushed and shuffled from side to side.

"Well I wouldn't say no. I mean he *is* attractive. He's got a nice body."

"So you've seen him shirtless then?"

"NO! I TOLD YOU WE AREN'T HAVING IT OFF." I ignored her needless rage.

"You don't have to be having it off to see someone shirtless. You could have seen him at the beach or…"

"Yeah! Saw him at the beach didn't I." Why did she say that only *after* I had made the suggestion? It could have been an innocent slipping of the thoughts but I sensed not. I sensed she was trying to hide something.

"Which beach was this?"

"It were when we were on holiday in Marbella." She pronounced it 'Mar-Bellor.'

"I'm guessing, since you aren't together, that you went as a group. Who else went?"

"There was Rhyddian, his girlfriend Carla…" She paused for an age, a clear sign she was making this up. "Then there was Tommy… Oh and Manuel!" Manuel? She went on holiday to Spain with someone called *Manuel*? She was *definitely* making this up, or the names at least.

Either she and Rhyddian went alone or not at all.

"I suppose that since you went on holiday together you and Carla get on well? What does she think of the rumour that you and her boyfriend are having it off? I'm presuming she knows because you wouldn't want her to get the wrong end of the stick, would you?"

"She finds it quite funny," Chalmers laughed for a brief moment and I took the opportunity to jump tracks.

"Tell me about Dewi Croft, Miss Chalmers."

"Dewi Croft? He the man who were here yesterday? Yeah... I didn't like him."

"And why not?"

"He was going to lose me my job and I wouldn't have got no good reference from him neither."

"Do you have ambitions Miss Chalmers? Do you want to work for a high class magazine or newspaper. *Pravda* say."

Don't ask me why I said Pravda. I have no idea why I said Pravda. It was the first newspaper that sprang to mind.

"Pravda? Like what the devil wears in that film? No... Not Pravda. I hated that film." Oh God! I wanted to strangle her for her stupidity. "But I would like to work somewhere like *OK* or *Hello*…"

"Cosmopolitan?" It was a better suggestion than Pravda.

"Isn't that an ice cream?" I'm sure I would have been forgiven for some old fashioned police brutality but I refrained from slapping her silly and moved on with my line of questioning.

"Tell me, Miss Chalmers, what do you know of a certain urban legend about Welshmen in the city after midnight?" She looked mighty confused so I elaborated further. "It's rumoured that it is legal to shoot a Welshman with a bow and arrow within the city walls after midnight." The face of Francesca Chalmers was priceless.

"Really? You can do that?" She paused. "Not that *I'd* be able to do it anyway. I'm useless with a bow and arrow." Note that she told me straight up that she wasn't very good, as if she were trying to divert suspicion away from herself.

"You tried it on your team building weekend a couple of years ago, I believe?"

"Yeah. I was no good but Rhyddian and Ben Jarmin were ace!"

Rhyddian?

Well that *was* interesting. Barnard had downplayed his skill and Guinness had said that he hadn't been very good at archery. I sensed at the time that Guinness had been lying and Francesca Chalmers had just proved it, that is if she herself wasn't lying, and she didn't appear to be on this occasion.

"Do you know a man named Cole Spencer? Works at the Grosvenor?"

"Cole!" She said his name as though she were surprised to hear me mention it. "No… I don't know Cole Spencer." She said the last part in such a solemn, childlike way that I *knew* she was lying.

"I think you *do* know Cole Spencer Miss Chalmers. Tell me. How do you know him? Is it through Rhyddian Barnard?"

"I *don't* know Cole Spencer," Chalmers bawled. I grumbled, knowing once again that she was lying to me. She seemed like a pathological liar but she was as good at lying as Boris Johnson. She had lied about the candlelit dinner and the holiday to 'Mar-bella' and now she had lied about knowing Cole Spencer.

"If you're lying I can easily find out Miss Chalmers. Cole Spencer is sitting in a cell down in the police station and I can easily ask him if *he* knows you or Rhyddian Barnard. Miss Chalmers, if you *are* lying you're looking at a perversion charge. So which is it to be?" Francesca Chalmers looked at me, wide eyed and frightened. Then she dared to defy to the law.

"I don't know Cole Spencer!"

I finished off by interviewing the rest of the staff, who gave me no information other than that they thought Dewi Croft was a decent enough man, that they thought Francesca Chalmers and Rhyddian Barnard were having it off with each other and that Rhyddian Barnard had been a fair shot during the team building weekend.

I also had everything they told me confirmed by the receptionist downstairs. It turned that Mr Guinness *was* lying after all, perhaps to protect one of his prize reporters. It hadn't done him any good in the end. Most of the staff knew about the urban legend and once I had collected their addresses and photographs from the receptionist I made my way back to the station with the intent of dropping into Corwen's office along the way.

My visit to the Gazette had yielded leads so I came out feeling like I was getting somewhere close to the killer. If I were allowed to put money on the killer I would have placed it on Rhyddian Barnard. He was decent with a bow and he had the motive of potentially losing his job behind him. I also suspected he knew Cole Spencer.

There was also the matter of his location.

Duke Street was not far from the walls and not far from the spot where Dewi Croft was killed *but* it *was* south from Eastgate and I was convinced no sane person would dare traverse Newgate at night. Barnard seemed too sensible to try such a thing. Barnard, if he were the killer, would have had to have run to the canal and then doubled back on himself after disposing of the weapon and he would have had to have doubled back on himself by quite a long way. It didn't seem right somehow. It seemed illogical. The easiest thing for Barnard to do would be to dispose of the weapon in the river and that meant crossing Newgate, which I knew was too foolish and idiotic to be plausible. He didn't seem like the sort to be that stupid.

I stopped at the end of Watergate and took out my phone, pressing Corwen's speed dial.

"Yo Pops," he chirruped as he answered.

"I'm outside your office. Any chance of a cuppa?"

"Sure. Glenda is already on her way down so she'll let you in."

Corwen hung up at the same time as I saw a curious and old fashioned brown door, hardly noticed by the throngs of shoppers, open up in the wall of the row beside the '*Hair café.*' Out of it came Glenda, a bright and pleasant enough girl. We exchanged greetings and pleasantries before I passed through the door and into a dank tunnel running parallel to the northern part of Bridge Street.

It's a service tunnel for the shops on Bridge Street, a place for deliveries and what not, but sometimes it's used an easy access for private rooms on the upper floors. Corwen's office was one of these and the office door, which was usually unlocked, was only a short way down the alley.

Then up the narrow, winding staircase to the top floor, clinging onto the handrail all the way. I can't begin to tell you how much I hate that staircase. It's so steep that climbing it is like scaling the north face of the Eiger and coming down again so perilous that I feel I need a safety harness and abseiling equipment.

At my age it takes longer than it should to reach the office at the top and I'm always breathless when Luke hands me a cup of tea (always in an antique William Gladstone shaped mug) as I fall through the door at the top.

Luke had only come to Chester a few years ago, around the same time as all the business with King Harold started, but since then he had become Corwen's best friend and the two were now inseparable.

He looks like an absolute tit. He has this lengthy, unkempt brown hair and one of those ridiculous tufts under his lip. Those ridiculous tufts seem to be all too common these days and I can't explain why. The man who did the singing at Will's wedding had the same sort thing and he looked just as ridiculous.

I mean, if you're going to grow something on your face at

least make an effort and grow something reasonable. A goatee at the very least, not just a ridiculous tuft of hair under your lip.

Despite looking like an idiot, Luke isn't a bad sort. He seems a bit quiet at first but once he opens his mouth he can talk for England, and without babbling too would you believe. He's quite clever but you'd never know that by looking at him.

"Morning Mr P," he chirruped as I opened the door, handing me a freshly steaming tea in my usual mug. I took it and fell into a chair.

"Can't you put in a lift or something? Those stairs are lethal." Luke laughed.

"Sorry. The council won't let us. Something about listed building regulations."

"Can't you plead that you need it for disabled access?"

"We've tried but because we don't meet clients up here they say it isn't necessary. We don't have any disabled staff either so…"

"Can't you hire somebody who's disabled then? Or better still… Break both of someone's legs!" I sipped at my tea, seething at those stairs.

"Hey Pops," Corwen strolled into the room, looking through a pile of papers. "Colman… Did we ever find out who that Russian was? The one who sounded a bit like an over the top Bond villain?"

"Putin!" Colman replied. Corwen nodded and threw the pile of papers into a nearby bin.

"In that case we'll ignore him as a conflict of interests."

I always liked their attitude to work. They were selective about their clients and they only took on the jobs which they found to be most beneficial. According to Corwen an awful lot was thrown their way but most of the time it was all dismissed. Every so often, usually around November, the company tried poaching me but I always refused. Working in the same office as Corwen would be too much and I'm far too old and far too happy with my station in life to change it now.

"Did you look into that legal business?" I asked. Corwen pulled up a chair, settling his feet on the desk in front.

"As you said this morning, it's a common urban legend. Not just here but across the country. Almost every town along the Welsh borders has something about it. Trouble is that we can't find any actual trace of the law ever being enacted anywhere. And, get this, to our knowledge this is the first time such a thing has *ever* happened."

"Interesting. So if it was never enacted and there is no precedent then we *could* bring it up as straight murder." I grinned over the lip of my mug.

"Maybe. But the idea *had* to come from somewhere," Luke pointed out. "Most urban legends have a basis in truth. Take the thing with King Harold." I squinted at him. I have often suspected that Corwen and Luke were involved in the King Harold fiasco somewhere along the line but I've never managed to prove it. I pushed the idea of King Harold away and went back to the legal matter.

"So… Basically… What you're saying is that if we can find some evidence of where this urban legend comes from we may find a way of getting round it?"

"We've already done some digging," Corwen added. "From what we found the idea of this law goes back to 1403 and maybe had something to do with the Glyndwr uprising. Apparently Prince Hal made the order to protect the city from attack, but so far we haven't found any documentary proof that the order was ever made."

"However… We did come across something that *might* be evidence the order did exist… The rows!" I stared at Luke with a curious eye.

"What have the rows got to do with it?"

"The rows are unique. It's been argued by some academics that they were created as an extra and practical means of defence for the city should anybody, say the Welsh, ever get beyond the walls. And seeing as they were created somewhere between 1293 and 1356 it fits with that period when the Welsh were rebelling against English rule."

"There were rebellions in 1287, 1294 and 1316 as well as the Glyndwr in 1400," Corwen added.

"Then explain that building dated 1274 at the end of Bridge Street," I snarked.

"That building may not have originally been part of the rows. It may have been integrated into them at a later date."

"And what physical proof is there that the rows were built to provide an ideal hunting ground for Welshmen?"

"Well there's the rows themselves of course… Just take a

look at them."

"So why don't any of the other places which claim the law have similar structures? Surely if Chester had come up with this unique defensive strategy then it would have been exported to other places. And why didn't every other defended medieval city adopt the same idea?" Corwen and Luke gave each other a sad look and then both turned away from me, knowing I was right. "Have you found anything else that might be useful?" It was Luke who answered me.

"Well… We did find out that only English people were allowed to live inside the garrison towns. You know, Conwy and Caernarfon. It's possible that this rule was applied to the border towns as well. So maybe Welsh people weren't allowed to live inside the walls."

"Perhaps then," I smiled, "if there was a ban on Welsh people living inside the city walls there were also restrictions on when they could be wandering around. They must have been allowed in to trade I assume. Perhaps they were only allowed inside during daylight hours or otherwise face some sort of penalty. Killed on sight?"

"The only issue with that," Corwen said, "Is how you

would identify who was Welsh and who wasn't. It can't have been based purely on looks because that doesn't work. Some form of ID like a badge or an armband? Nah. No evidence. Accent? Possible but that doesn't apply to everyone. Not everybody who is Welsh has a Welsh accent. There's no way of telling. And with no way of telling everybody outside after dark would have had to have been stopped and questioned. If it was particularly busy, if there was a festival on or something, that would be almost impossible."

"Perhaps the curfew was general," Luke said. "Perhaps it was for everybody. Perhaps anybody was liable to be shot if found outside after dark. They *were* harsh times after all."

"That sounds possible," I said, draining the remainder of my tea and placing my Gladstone mug on a nearby window ledge. "Did you get anywhere on the legal contradiction aspect of this thing?"

"Yes… In a sense," Corwen responded. "In normal circumstances where laws are directly contradictory then it's the latter law that takes precedence. Under the homicide act of fifty seven this could be classed as wilful murder and you'd get a conviction without a problem. However... Everything in this case depends on the phrasing of the law. We know that murder was punishable by death in medieval times and so it might be the case that the actual law, should it exist, may contain a clause which makes conviction impossible."

"So it could say something like: 'You may shoot any Welshman found at large in the city after curfew and shoot him without charge or penalty under the common law of England?' If it says that then you'll never get a conviction as the clause specifically states you can get away with it."

I glowered at the wall. If the law contained such a clause, which having studied law I would have said was unfortunately likely, then we were up a certain creek without a paddle.

I left the company of Corwen and Luke to return to the police station. The main CID room was buzzing as I entered and Baskin, who was pouring over some papers, looked up and waved me over.

"What have you got for me?" I asked, pulling up a chair next to him.

"This is a list of calls and texts from Cole Spencer's mobile in the last seven days." He showed me the top paper. "The bad news is that he hasn't used it since yesterday evening." I was dumbfounded for a moment.

"What? But the CCTV clearly shows him calling somebody on a mobile phone!"

"Yes... On *a* mobile phone but not *his* mobile phone."

"So whose mobile was it if not his?"

"According to the phone company the mobile that made the call at that time is registered to Elsie MacGonagall." I nodded my head and scratched my chin.

"Maybe Spencer took MacGonagall's mobile phone from somewhere, maybe from behind the reception desk, and slipped it back after making the call. Tell you what... Go back to the hotel CCTV and see if you can track Spencer's movements for the two hours before the murder and until the police arrive. Log exactly where he goes and what he does. You might find him taking the phone."

I started to walk away but Baskin called me back.

"There is something else sir... There's a number Cole Spencer seems to call regularly, as late as yesterday, but it doesn't seem to be on his contacts list."

"Who does it belong to?" I asked, trying to contain my excitement.

It didn't take much of a leap to assume that the reason the number had been removed from the address book was because he was trying to disassociate himself with that person. There are a number of reasons why you might disassociate yourself with someone, you may have a falling out, but seeing as this disassociation must surely have been recent it would have been a coincidence if it had been a falling out.

No... The fact that calls to that number had been made recently demonstrated one thing and one thing only. That number *had* to be the number of the killer for why else would Cole Spencer disassociate himself from that person?

It was another attempt to make him appear as an innocent party and not the accomplice he was. His recent calls and contacts had been deleted and he had called someone using

Elsie MacGonagall's phone prior to the murder. If that had been an entirely innocent phone call why not use his own phone?

The answer was that it *wasn't* an innocent phone call. Spencer was trying to deflect suspicion from himself but like all criminals who attempt to outsmart the law he had undershot his target. The mere act of deflecting suspicion from himself was in itself suspicious and by doing it Cole Spencer had left himself and his accomplice wide open to capture.

"I've got Reeves running a check on the number now," Baskin i.

"Good. Once you have it check it against the number that was called from Elsie MacGonagall's phone last night. If they're one and the same, as I assume they were, then we almost certainly have our killer."

I went to my desk confident that the murderer was within my grasp, noting another message on my photo frame mentioning that the divers had found no trace of a weapon in the canal.

I sat staring at a map of the city on the wall for what only seemed a few seconds but actually, in the end, turned out to be ten minutes and I was thinking the whole time.

Dewi Croft had been shot from Eastgate. The murderer then ran along to the canal to dispose of the murder weapon. Then they had escaped.

Or had they?

A crazy, out of nowhere thought struck me.

I had been assuming that the killer had gone to the canal because that was the logical way to go. Only a fool would cross Newgate in the dark, as I kept saying.

But what if the killer hadn't been logical at all? What if they had decided to tackle Newgate in the dark? The divers hadn't found any murder weapon in the canal, yet, so it stood to reason that, if the murder weapon wasn't there, it must have been thrown into the river instead. That meant that either the murderer was an absolute imbecile or Newgate was his quickest and easiest option of escaping from the scene of the crime.

If it *was* his quickest option then that suggested he was based south of the crime scene. There was nowhere else he *could* be based *if* he had crossed Newgate. Nobody who was based *north* of the crime scene, not even a fool, would bother to brave Newgate if they didn't have to, not for any feasible reason. Anywhere east could be discounted too because it would still have been easier to run to the canal and leave the wall near the cathedral. There was little to the west apart from the racecourse and most of the city centre.

So if the killer was based over in that direction, again, the logical direction to run would be to the north, to the canal. The only reason for crossing Newgate at all would be if the killer was based somewhere close to it.

And, also, the killer *must* have been based a short distance from the scene of the crime. You don't want to be waiting for a bus after committing a murder and deploying a taxi would add an unnecessary witness. A taxi driver would be able to finger the killer. The killer *could* have driven into the city but then why chance Newgate when there was no need? Besides, there is plenty of parking north of Newgate. Once again, there was little need to chance it. Plus any cars driving about the city at that time of night would be easily identified. It was too risky a strategy considering the nature of the crime. He *had* to have done everything on foot.

All of this narrowed the killer's base of operations. Whoever it was had to be based somewhere south of Newgate, a not too considerable distance from Eastgate. That made the process of the whole crime so ridiculously easy to deduce, especially considering what I already knew.

After Dewi Croft left the hotel Cole Spencer contacted the killer (Perhaps using Elsie MacGonagall's phone. I made a note to check up on that later). The killer then ran to Eastgate and waited for the return of Dewi Croft, a return signalled by Cole Spencer as he re-entered the hotel after his secret rendezvous with Elsie MacGonagall. A rendezvous I became sure was only intended to provide Spencer with an alibi. There was only a limited time frame available for the killer to get from wherever they were based to Eastgate. Dewi Croft could have returned from his walk at any moment, despite what he had told Elsie MacGonagall about returning in half an hour. The killer had to be based within a five minutes of Eastgate at the most and that put them in a very small space to the north of the river but still south of Newgate.

There wasn't a lot down that way. There were the Roman

gardens and the groves. All of the houses in that part of the city were inside the walls (more or less) and there were less than two hundred of them. I also supposed that it was the case that the killer had to be within easy reach of the wall, say a few minutes away at the most. That would, in theory, place the killer between Lower Bridge Street and the wall. Once more the killer's base narrowed. Most of that space was taken up by shops and a multi storey car park and there weren't so many residences around there. Less than fifty or maybe a little more. Most of the residences were around Albion Street and Duke Street with a few flats above the shops on lower Bridge Street…

For the only time in my entire career I was struck by a flash of divine revelation.

I knew exactly who the killer was and how the whole thing had played out. The crime was daring and opportunistic but it had relied on chance. It had relied on us assuming that nobody would try and cross Newgate in the dark, which we *had* initially done, and it had relied on us assuming that the weapon had been disposed of in the canal. But as was usually the case our killer had been too damn smart for his own good. He had failed to consider that once we found the canal was a dead end the only other option was the river and we would check it. And by running down that way, as I have described, it narrowed the range of what was possible. It narrowed the escape possibilities. Most of all, it pointed to the killer as though his confession were written in blood on his own forehead. It made things all too easy.

I knew everything.

I sprang from my chair and rushed over to Baskin, who was sifting through paperwork.

"Has Reeves got that number yet?" I asked. Baskin shook his head. "Well I know who it is." I wrote the name down on a sheet of paper along with a few other details. "Dredge the river and you'll find the weapon. And I'm certain if you check the CCTV footage from Lower Bridge Street from shortly after the murder he *will* be there."

I left Baskin befuddled and skipped to the cells to once

more confront Cole Spencer. There were only three cells in our small station and Spencer's was the only one occupied. I opened the hatch, looked through and saw him pacing the floor with an angry look on his face. He turned around and glared with irritation and disdain back through the hole in the door. I closed it again and unlocked the door, striding inside without trying to look too smug.

"What do you want?" Spencer snapped. "Unless you've come to release me why don't you clear off?"

"No. I've not come to release you. I've come to find out where you were before you started work last night." Spencer screwed his eyes up. They were red and puffed up.

"I was at home," he said bitterly.

"What about before that? Say around four or five?" There was silence. "You met up with a friend didn't you? You met up with the same friend you contacted just before the murder of Dewi Croft?" Again, silence. I folded my arms. "You know if you cooperate with us you'll have an easier ride? Of course, you'll still have to spend time in prison but not so much. Maybe they'll give you two years with a chance of parole after one and maybe they'll let you go to one with lighter security. I hear the minimum security prisoners aren't so big on the conjugal comradeship, if you get my meaning.

"I'm not afraid of that," Spencer bluffed. It sounded, from the tone of his voice, that he didn't actually understand what I had said and he was putting on a tough face, deluding himself in the hope it would deter me.

"Let me put my question another way. Did you speak to anyone before going to work? Did you call someone from home? Did you message anyone?" Spencer sneered and did not answer. "If you didn't speak to anyone or meet with anyone then how did you plan the murder? I know It must have been planned to some degree and I know you were in on it, Spencer." Spencer's eyes widened worriedly as I began to push him up against the metaphorical ropes. He knew he was beaten and he knew I had the case almost tied up. He knew, at last, that there was no point in hiding the truth any more and so he began to confess everything.

They always crack in the end.

I had an officer attend to Spencer so that he could write his statement and then set out from the station to collect those final pieces of the puzzle.

I pounded across the road, filled with afternoon shoppers, towards St Werburgh street and then up the little path besides the cathedralwhich took me up onto the walls.

I slipped under the cordon at Eastgate and flashed my badge to the officer on duty, explaining that I was following a lead. I stopped under the clock tower and looked down at the similarly cordoned off area in front of the Grosvenor. Two constables were walking the street looking for anyone who might have seen anything suspicious the night before but I doubted they would have any luck. On the other side of the gate another constable was trying to appease some angry tourists and for a moment I had to help explain to them that the walls were closed as part of an ongoing enquiry but would. It took five minutes to convince them but they *were* convinced in the end and walked off whilst grousing about the pointlessness of police procedure.

I waited a good few minutes, asking the constable about similar incidents throughout the day, and then pressed on towards Newgate at a comfortable pace. It was more of a distance than I had thought and I considered this as I walked along the narrow wall, past the ugly multi-storey care park and the even uglier *NFU* building before arriving at Newgate.

The stone steps up to the top were well worn and decidedly treacherous but making matters worse was the fact that they weren't exactly straight. They curved just a tad and this only added to their treachery. It really was a foolish idea of the killer's to cross this in the dark. I stopped at the top and looked out over Pepper Street, towards the amphitheatre, the *Travel Lodge* opposite and the church of St John the Baptist at the head of Grosvenor Park. There was one of those open topped 'city sightseeing buses' heading down the road, filled with tourists, furiously snapping away at the amphitheatre but ignoring the church until their audio guides casually informed them that it was rumoured to be the last resting place of King Harold. At this point they all turned and began to furiously take as many pictures as possible before it passed from view.

I carried on up the wall.

On the far side of Newgate I took the first opportunity to get back down to street level, the steps being immediately next to the gate, and I walked along Park Street to the *Albion Inn*. It is a nicely old fashioned place on the corner that looked like a left over set piece from a film about the Victorian East End. On the outside it looks to be tiny, cramped and crowded but this is deceptive as it is much roomier than it first appears. Luke and Corwen once tried to jokingly explain to me that the pub is 'dimensionally transcendental' and really *is* bigger on the inside but I didn't fall for it.

It was mostly empty apart from one grizzled old alcoholic nursing a half empty pint glass and a large, balding man in a black shirt languishing behind the bar whilst half-heartedly cleaning some glasses with a ragged cloth. He placed this down and nodded as I approached.

"Alright mate. What can I get you?"

I took out my badge and flashed it.

"D.S Proctor. Do you mind if I ask you about two people who were in here yesterday evening?"

"No. Go ahead," he smiled. I reached into my pocket and pulled out a picture of Cole Spencer.

"This man... Was he in here yesterday evening?" The man took the photo from my grasp and gazed at it.

"Aye. I know him. Comes in here regularly. Usually with a few friends." He handed the photo back.

"Was he in here yesterday evening?" This time the man gave me a direct answer.

"Aye. He was in here with a friend."

"Can you describe this friend to me?" The barman gave an exact description of the person Spencer had fingered. "What did they do whilst they were here? What was their attitude?"

"When they came in they both looked a bit gloomy. They ordered their pints and then went and sat in the corner over there." He pointed nonchalantly and I looked to an empty table tucked away in the corner.

"And what about once seated? What were they like then?"

"I can't say I really noticed. They only stayed for about an hour and then left."

"Did they appear conspiratorial at all? Did they look like they were planning something?" The barman looked intrigued for a second.

"Now you mention it they were looking a little shifty before they left. They had their heads together and were talking in whispers, like they were plotting something." I made a movement of my head and smiled, taking out a second photo.

"Was it this person?"

"Aye. It was."

"Ok. Thank you. I presume we can find you here if we need anything more from you?" The man nodded cautiously and I smiled before bidding him good day.

Cole Spencer and his friend were seen conspiring in the Albion. I thought that it shouldn't make much difference to the final case but it was still needed just one more piece and the thing was done.

I took the road along the wall towards the river and then turned onto Duke Street.

Duke Street is like the whole city in microcosm. At one end you had the walls and all along its length there is a hodgepodge of modern and ancient architecture ranging from battered mews houses occupied by students to ugly concrete and brick office buildings. The place I was looking for was an unassuming terrace somewhere towards the far end. On the outside the house looked small with a bright yellow door and two oddly positioned windows on the upper and lower floors. Unless it was another dimensionally transcendental building it was probably just as small on the inside.

I wasted no time finding out and marched to the door, knocking so hard that I scratched the paintwork.

It was opened by a woman, somewhere in her late twenties, in a silk kimono style dressing gown embroidered with little black dragons. It was quite an admirable piece of clothing although I must say it hardly suited *her*. She looked like she was expecting a booty call. She was not what I would call overweight but she was bulky and her size wasn't improved by the fact that her breasts must have been, at a rough guess, a double G cup.

The reason I know this is because when I was married to Anna she used to send me bra shopping, about three times a year as a means of getting in touch with my feminine side. It never worked and its only achievement was that I always ended up buying the sexiest lingerie in the store and learning more than was necessary about bra sizes.

Anna was never happy about the sexy lingerie.

"Yes? Can I help you?" the lady irked. I smiled and held up my police ID.

"Carla Naismith? I'm D.S Simon Proctor, city police. May I come in?" Carla looked worried.

"What is this about?"

"I'm making enquiries into a serious incident and I'd like to ask you a few questions, if I may." Carla fussed and twitched before she finally agreed and moved aside so I could enter.

The place *was* small and there was barely enough room to swing a cat but that also meant that it wasn't hard to find the lounge. I was unapologetically seating myself in a comfortable armchair by the front window.

"Would you like a cup of tea Mr Proctor?" Carla asked from the door.

"If there is one on the go then yes, that would be lovely. No sugar, milk second- Thank you." I always feel I have to tell people this last one. Tea with the milk in first always tastes weaker because the maker pours far too much in and ruins the whole cup. It's a bone of contention and some people become offended by the way I prefer my tea but Carla, although she seemed a bit disturbed my request, took it in her stride.

Whilst she was in the kitchen I took the opportunity to do a sortie of the room to see if I could find anything of interest. There were many women's magazines, a copy of *Tess of The D'Urbervilles* by Thomas Hardy and several pictures which were all of Carla and Rhyddian Barnard.

I was looking at one on the mantle above the fireplace when Carla came back with the tea.

"My boyfriend… Rhyddian," she said as she handed me a cup.

"Yes… We've met. He's the reason I'm here." Carla once

again became agitated and she flopped down onto the sofa.

"He's not in trouble is he?" I took my first sip of the tea and decided that it was decent enough. Not perfect but decent.

"That depends, Miss Naismith. If your information tallies with his then he may not."

"*May* not?"

"My colleagues are currently following up another line of inquiry that may turn up evidence against him," I said. Carla looked alarmed. "Now if you don't mind I'd like to get straight down to business and ask you about last night."

"Of course. Go Ahead," Carla said, albeit reluctantly.

"Was Rhyddian here last night?"

"Yes."

"And what time did he arrive? Approximately?"

"It was just gone half six. He said he was coming so I put some tomato sauce on the stove."

"You make your own tomato sauce?"

"Oh yes. I try to make as much as I can myself." She sounded proud of this. "If I make it myself at least I know what's in it."

"So what did the two of you do when Rhyddian arrived?"

"Nothing much. I wanted to go out somewhere but Rhyddian claimed he wasn't in the mood. He'd had a bad day at work and he'd already had a drink with a friend from work beforehand I think but he didn't say who it was."

"Did he tell you *why* he'd had a bad day?"

"He said something about a takeover and that he may lose his job but that was all. He doesn't really talk about work."

"What about the articles he writes? Does he show them to you?"

"I read them when they get printed in the paper but he never shows them to me."

"And what about Francesca Chalmers? I understand you're both friends? Does she ever talk about work when the two of you meet up?" Carla pulled a puzzled face.

"Francesca Chalmers? No… We're not friends."

"Oh. I'm sorry. I must have been misled. I was told you and Rhyddian went on holiday with her to Marbella…."

"Marbella? No. I've never been to Marbella. Rhyddian went on a stag party there once but…" She stopped suddenly and a second later her hand went to her mouth and tears started to form in her eyes.

"Are you okay?" I reached over and put a hand on her knee. She smiled and wiped away the tears, pretending everything was fine, even though I knew that it wasn't.

"I'm fine," she lied. "But if you wouldn't mind just getting on with your questions."

"So what did you do instead of going out?"

"We ate our meal, watched some TV. *Coast* I think. And then we watched a film, *The Black Cauldron.* I really wanted to watch *Saturday Night Fever* but Rhyddian was dead against it."

"Ninety minutes of John Travolta dancing like a tit. I saw it when it first came out. You aren't missing much," I said. "What did the two of you do after the film?" Carla blushed the colour of scarlet but she still answered, albeit a little more timidly.

"Rhyddian wanted to have sex. We went to sleep after that."

"And Rhyddian was still here this morning?"

"Yes."

"And he didn't leave the house during the night?"

"I don't think so." Carla became very confused. "He was still in bed when I woke up this morning."

"Did *you* leave the house during the night?"

"No!"

"Did you or Rhyddian wake up in the night at all?"

"I can't tell you about Rhyddian but I know *I* definitely didn't wake up." I urged her to elaborate further for the sake of the investigation. "I have an insomniac disorder. I need to take sleeping tablets in order to combat it."

"So you'd have been out cold *all night* then?"

"Yes."

"So you couldn't possibly know if Rhyddian went out? It could be possible that he slipped out of bed and came back later on and you would never know?" Carla slowly nodded to show it were true, becoming more and more worried with each question.

"Could I see these sleeping tablets?" I asked quietly.

She was gone for an awfully long time and when she returned she was pale and shaking. I stood up and put a hand to her shoulder.

"Are you alright Miss Naismith?" She nodded and

flumped down onto the sofa, still shaking.

The sleeping pills were in her hand. I gently prized them from between her fingers and examined them closely, dropping a few into my hands to look at them more closely and carefully reading everything on the bottle. They were powerful little buggers. Would have definitely knocked her out for the night. Miss Naismith wouldn't have known a thing of what was going on around her and Barnard could have slipped in and out of bed without her ever noticing.

"You're an archer I understand?" Carla nodded slowly. She didn't look at me. "Do you practice regularly?"

"Yes. I'm still a member of the university archery club."

"But you're no longer a student?"

"No."

Not a student but still a member of their club? People who do that bug the hell out of me and always have done. Whilst I was at university there was at least one of that sort in each society and in some cases these people were over forty, married and had school age children. There was one particularly irritating man at my student newspaper, I won't name and shame, whom I desperately wanted to punch in the face and order to go and move on with his life rather than hanging around a university where all the students had only just been in infant school at the time when he had been graduating. According to a friend of mine who studied for a PhD he was still there by the time he achieved his doctorate and even, apparently, for a few years beyond that. He's probably still there now, all old and retired and still desperately clinging to his student days in what I can only describe as a pathetic state of affairs.

Had Carla not been looking so peaky by this point I would have gently advised her to remove herself from the precincts of the university and move on with her life. There is a time when we all must move on and hers was definitely past. But given her state, saying something was not appropriate.

"What kind of arrows do you use?" I asked, thinking I knew the answer. She stumbled her words so I made my guess. "They wouldn't by any chance be green fletched 32' steel tipped fibreglass arrows?" I was right on the money. Carla's eyes widened.

"Could I see your bow Miss Naismith?"

She agreed, stood up and promptly fainted.

Whilst waiting for the ambulance to arrive I did a sweep of the house. I had no warrant but as I suspected that I would not find what I was looking for I felt that one was not necessary.

There was no bow in the house but I did find an unopened pack of green fletched arrows, freshly delivered from Ebay, of the same type which killed Mr Croft, in the under stairs cupboard. I covered myself to my superiors by claiming I was looking for a mop with which to wipe up a spillage Carla had created when she fainted and had accidentally come across the arrows in the process. They believed me, thank goodness.

After calling the ambulance a phone call from Reeves confirmed everything. Divers had found Carla Naismith's bow in the river and it was already being swabbed for fingerprints. CCTV footage of lower bridge street had also revealed the killer returning from the scene of the crime.

The footage was clear too, so clear that there was little doubt as to his identity.

It was all the evidence that was needed to make an arrest and when Rhyddian Barnard turned up at the house on Duke Street, at the same time as the ambulance, I slapped a pair of cuffs to his wrists and had him dragged down to the station.

He confessed everything.

Following the news that he was likely to lose his job as the result of Dewi Croft's takeover, he and Cole Spencer had met in the Albion and there came up with the plan to kill Croft by shooting him after midnight, Carla's need for sleeping pills providing Rhyddian with the perfect opportunity to leave and return to Duke Street unnoticed. They also reckoned that Barnard could easily dispose of the weapon in the river, mostly for the convenience of it, but also because they assumed that we would never look there. They rightly guessed that we would make the assumption that only a fool would dare to cross Newgate in the dark and head off in the wrong direction to search the canal.

What happened next was pure opportunism.

Dewi Croft had played right into their hands by going for a late night stroll. Had he not then Spencer would have called Barnard to Eastgate then lured Croft from the hotel under some pretence that there was a gentleman outside who urgently wished to speak to him. The moment he stepped through the door Barnard, lying in wait, would have killed him and ran to dispose of the weapon in the river. Spencer would have waited ten minutes before pretending to have discovered the body (unless somebody else had done so first) and he would provide us, the police, with a generic description of the man wanting to speak to Mr Croft, sending us on another wild goose chase.

But Mr Croft's late night walk changed the plan. It let Spencer use Elsie Macgonagall as his patsy, her absence buying cigarettes placing her squarely in the frame as the killer. The framing was supported by the use of MacGonagall's phone to signal Croft's return to Barnard.

It played into their hands, but it made convicting them so much easier.

Barnard and Spencer had been far too clever for their own good. They thought that by shooting Mr Croft from the walls it would make escape easy and detection impossible. They thought it meant they could dispose of the weapon and we would never find it.

They were wrong.

From the start Thomlinson and I had figured it was near impossible for Elsie MacGonagall to have committed the crime. The whole idea was far too convoluted to be plausible. There was no way that she could have worked as the killer. They had forgotten about the CCTV cameras, not just on the street but in the hotel too. It had slipped their minds that in the modern world nothing goes unnoticed. Everything every person does is watched and if we sin there is no escaping justice. It was a fundamental slip and it damned them both.

Despite his full confession Rhyddian Barnard was adamant that he had not broken the law. He was certain that no court in the land would convict him for what he claimed was a well-known 'loophole' and he claimed that he was within his legal right to kill a Welshman in Chester after midnight. Again, he was being a too clever for his own good. He thought that by exploiting this 'loophole' he could get away with cold blooded murder but there was no way anybody in the legal system would let that happen. Murder is murder and that *is* a crime, no matter what some urban legend says.

In the police station we came up with a loophole of our own which we could exploit to legitimise our arrest if necessary, though it never came to that thank goodness. We would argue that Barnard was guilty of murder regardless. He wasn't *within* the walls. He was *on* them. It was a technicality and it would have been a difficult thing to argue for in court but, as I say, it never came to that.

Whether that law about Welshmen ever existed or not I do not know, but there is no record of it on the statute books it turns out. So, with no record, the killing of Dewi Croft was presented to the courts as cold blooded murder.

Rhyddian Barnard was sentenced to life imprisonment. A month into his sentence his cell was found empty. How he escaped remains unknown.

As for Carla Naismith? My line of questioning (specifically my mentioning of the holiday to Marbella) had brought her around to the realisation that Barnard and

Francesca Chalmers had been having an affair and this is what had brought about her fit of pique. Once she recovered she was fine and she stormed from the Countess of Chester Hospital to nearby Blacon police station where Barnard had been taken following his confession (A CSO had escorted her to the hospital and had informed her of the news).

The woman was like a force nine gale, refusing to leave until she had learned all she wanted to know about both the murder and Barnard's affair with Francesca Chalmers. The long nowhere relationship between those two lovers who had met at university ended that day and Carla Naismith was taken home in distress. She also gave up practising archery not long after. It reminded her too much of Barnard, too much of how they met and too much of his hateful crime.

And the other folk involved in this case? Francesca Chalmers skipped town when the news of Barnard's arrest was released to the press later that evening. It was such a shame as I would have really liked to have her hauled up before a judge for denying she knew Cole Spencer. She later wrote to Carla apologising for her affair with Barnard but it was not accepted. The last I heard she had ended up working as a fashion writer for an English Language newspaper in Djibouti.

The rest of the folks who worked at the Deva Gazette did not fare so well either. The paper never recovered from the scandal that was created by the news that one of its staff had killed the man who was take over and it went into administration a few months later. The editor, Mr Guinness, couldn't bear the shame and took his own life in a hotel suite at the Grosvenor, coincidentally the same as occupied by Dewi Croft and his wife.

Elsie Macgonagall was offered a job at the Ritz in London but she turned it down, preferring instead to remain at the Grosvenor where I understand that she is now in line for a fast track promotion to management.

Mirabel Croft flourished without her husband. She remarried six months later and *actually* divorced another six months after that. Something tells me she'll get through a lot more husbands before she is done.

Finally I come to the case of Cole Spencer and his words haunt me still. He was charged as an accomplice to murder and throughout his time in remand he remained utterly silent. The Monday following the crime he was placed before a magistrate at Chester Crown Court and spoke only three times, the first was to confirm his name and the second was to plead guilty. The third time was before being taken away to prison to await trial. He spoke clearly and with more confidence than I ever knew was possible.

"There will be others," he began. "In your eyes they shall be condemned as criminals but they shall be untouchable. They shall discover ways to break you, but in return they shall not be harmed. The very thing that condemns them shall become their protector. They shall come and they shall undermine the law itself. Their crimes shall be legal and there will be nothing you can do to stop them."

His voice echoed ominously around the courtroom and ever since that day I have not been able to sleep without dreaming of a crime ridden wasteland where no amount of policing or law could ever be effective, where every crime was legal.

Spencer was given a quite harsh ten years at his trial and he serves them without a word to his fellow inmates or gaolers.

Edgar House was a Georgian, luxury hotel up against the walls and it was Corwen who discovered they were offering elegant suppers at fifty pounds per head. I thought it a little too expensive but he assured me that Anna would love it when she came to visit. I argued but in the end, after walking past the place and noting that it had a good looking terrace which overlooked the walls and the river, I went inside and booked a table for three. I left with my wallet feeling empty and two days later Corwen dropped a major bombshell and followed it up by asking if I could book an extra place at the restaurant. It was another fifty pounds down the drain but I couldn't exactly say no. I declined from telling Anna in order to keep it a surprise.

And so, a few weeks after the archery murder case, I found myself sat alone watching the sun set over the river, sipping a glass of white wine on the terrace of Edgar House. I had been seated for ten minutes when I was aroused by a loud cry of: 'DAHLING!' from the gate.

I looked up from my glass to see Anna, arms wide and wearing a white dress and hat that, unsurprisingly, wouldn't have looked out of place on a let herself go a bit Audrey Hepburn. She planted a French kiss on both my cheeks.

"Dahling it's wonderful to see you," she said. "And still not looking your age I see. You do make me so jealous. You don't do anything to yourself whereas I've always worked so hard to keep my looks."

"At least you can afford to. There are plenty of women who have to settle for becoming fag hags," I said, mocking. Anna gently slapped my arms.

"Oh Simon you're such a tease… "

"Where are you staying this time around?" I asked as a waiter came to take Anna's order.

"A scotch for me, thank you dahling. I was going to stay at Rookery Hall near Nantwich but then I had the sudden urge to stay at the castle. You know how it is. If you've seen it once you *have* to see it again!" I knew the very feeling. "And of course, they're both so lovely and J.D is absolutely adorable. When he grows up he'll be a real heartbreaker like his dad. Claire too. I know she's only just over a year old but if I were her age I would be quite jealous."

"I hear from Corwen that they're expecting another one," I said.

"Yes. Due in February. That will mean three very young children running about the place. I don't think I could cope. Even one child is hard work. Do you remember the night we brought Corwen home from the hospital dahling? He screamed and howled all night and just plain refused to go to sleep!"

"Aye… And he's been keeping me awake at night ever since." The waiter came back with her scotch and she drew it from the tray with a smile and an air kiss.

"Is he still seducing the girls with Shakespeare quotes?"

"Yes. And they're getting worse by the week. It might not last for much longer though. That level of romantic seduction only works a few times on a girl at best." Anna's eyes twinkled.

"Simon… I do believe you're trying to tease me again. You aren't saying that Corwen has *finally* found a proper girlfriend are you?" I smiled and nodded. The secret was out.

"I don't know much about her yet. All I got out of Corwen was that she's older and they watched *Saturday Night Fever* together."

"What was it you used to call that film darling? Ninety minutes of John Travolta dancing like a tit?"

"The best thing about it was the music and you don't need to watch a bad film just to enjoy music."

"I think I saw it in New York with Otto and Claire," Anna said. Otto had been Anna's cousin and the original owner of the trilby which now lived with Corwen. "All three of us hated it. Claire and I stayed to the end to see how bad it got but Otto walked out half way through."

"I don't blame him."

"They were a lovely couple weren't they? Otto and Claire?"

This was one of the problems with Anna. She talked incessantly and she could ramble from one topic to the next without a break.

"He was fine when he was with her but when he was younger he was a royal pain in the arse. A right tearaway in desperate need of control. I remember Lilly once had one of those giant Barbie heads… You know the sort…" Never having had a sister or any kind of daughter I couldn't say that I did but, apparently, they were used for applying makeup and practising hairdressing and were a real girly girl sort of thing. "Well… One day Otto was bored and so he stole a chisel from the garage and then took the head from Lily whilst she was playing with it. She screamed bloody murder but that didn't stop Otto from being beastly. He made a hole in the mouth which he then stuck his schlong in and pretended the head was giving him a b-j!"

"How old was he?"

"Oh only about six or seven I think, but papa had already poisoned his mind with all manner of debauched ideas."

I had never known Anna's papa, Seamus, but he was a perfidious old rake by all accounts. It's no surprise that growing up in the same environment as such a man had turned Otto (and to a lesser extent, Anna, though she never lived with him on a permanent basis) towards some adult ideas and practices at an early age. Given how the family usually were when it came to such things, I only need to remind myself of some of the things I hear from Corwen whilst lying in bed at night, it was no surprise to learn the results of this.

"I suppose with Corwen finally getting a girlfriend he'll settle down like Otto did. Do you suppose there'll be a wedding? I know a lovely old dressmaker in dear Donostia and I've got this design that I'm just simply dying to have her make. Where do you suppose the ceremony will be? Somewhere nearby no doubt... Oh... Dahling! How about St John the Baptist? Not only is it lovely it's also got history!"

"I'd rather Corwen didn't get married there considering *who* is supposed to be buried nearby. And besides, shouldn't we give the relationship time to develop before talking of marriage?"

"You're such a spoilsport Simon. Always were. Where's your sense of adventure dahling?"

"I've had quite enough excitement for one year thank you very much," I scalded. Anna laughed.

"Oh yes. That frightful business with the man outside the Grosvenor. I forgot you were involved."

"Things could have gotten nasty had we not caught him. People would have assumed that you could get away with murder and it wouldn't be long before the lunatics were using all the tourists as target practice."

"It would certainly have been frightfully barbaric. But what was it that boy said in court? Something about breaking the law but being untouchable?"

"Yes. I think that was what he meant. He was a strange one…"

"You know all about the law darling. *Are* there any ways to break it and get away scot free?"

"Not to my knowledge. But if there *are* nobody is going to use them in my city. My job *is* and always *has* been to protect law and order. If I can't protect people under the law then I'll damn well protect them under the force of order. Crime or no crime you can't go around wreaking havoc with the lives of others just because you feel like it." Anna spread herself across the table and stared at me with puppy like eyes.

"Simon Proctor… Still the man I fell in love in with all those years ago!" I smiled.

"Yes but we both know you don't love me in the way you used to." Anna sat up and laughed.

"Oh don't be so silly Simon. Of course I still love you in the way I used to… Just not in the way I thought I did at the time!"

Her eyes fell to the door of the hotel and she let out a gasp of surprise.

"Oh my… She's not what I was expecting at all… She's rather a big girl, isn't she?"

I turned around to see Corwen and his new girlfriend walking towards us from the building. My jaw dropped and when they both reached the table the girl froze in recognition.

"Mam… Pops," Corwen announced. "This is…"

"I know," I told him. "CARLA NAISMITH!"

HEAR ME ROAR

EXHIBIT A: Panthera Onca

"For the final time," I snarled as I reached the top stair of Corwen's office, "there is *not* and never *has been* an escaped jaguar wandering around this city."

Pushing open the door to the office I hardly noticed the mug that Luke placed into my waiting hand.

"Are you absolutely *sure*, one hundred percent, that there's no escaped jaguar?" the journalist on the other end of the line asked. "Have you checked with Chester Zoo?"

"Yes. Myself and my ex-wife had a lovely day out with the wildebeest and I can assure you that all the zoo's jaguars are accounted for."

I flumped into a seat and put the mug down on the nearest desk, still not noticing it.

"What about Knowsley Safari Park?"

I had assumed journalists were educated people and yet here was this one asking if this imaginary jaguar had escaped from a safari park thirty miles away and had somehow got all the way to Chester without being seen.

"What about…"

"No private owner has reported a missing jaguar either," I snapped, giving the eye to Corwen and Luke who were in the corner of the room, giggling at my annoyance and trying to suppress their snickers like a couple of errant children.

"It could be an illegal... So they wouldn't report it, would they?"

"You think some... person... is going to lose something like a jaguar and not report it?" I lifted the mug and took a sip. The tea inside tasted strange, not like tea at all. I was so irritated by the conversation, actually, that I failed to register the fact that the tea was coffee.

"It has been known to happen, sir."

"Yes. It has. But not under my jurisdiction. This is no more than a childish rumour spread by internet trolls and wastrels."

"This rumour must have come from somewhere!"

"There is *no* escaped jaguar. Nor is there any other big cat wandering around the city. Now I suggest you go and find a proper news story. I'm sure there's one out there somewhere."

I slammed the phone off. Threw it to the desk.

You know how it is- Some tourist takes a picture and uploads it to the internet. Then somebody with too much imagination and no sense of logic or rationality sees a smudge in the background. Three minutes later, after zooming in and noticing that the smudge has a vague shape, they've deduced it's some sort of feline. A week later my inbox is flooded with supposed sightings of an escaped jaguar, an escaped jaguar wandering around the city centre, no less.

Forget the fact that if there was an escaped jaguar roaming the centre of Chester the whole world would have seen it and there would have been a panic as everybody ran for their lives, people were for some reason believing this rubbish.

I ask you, what happened to common sense? When did people become so unquestioning, so prone to accepting all the bullshit that gets hurled their way? Even journalists, educated people whose job it is to root out the truth, were jumping on this bandwagon.

I finally noticed the face staring at me from the front of the mug. Instead of Gladstone, as every right suggested it ought to have been, it was Earl Grey.

"Why am I drinking from Earl Grey?" I asked, taking another sip and also now noticing that it wasn't tea. "And why am I drinking coffee from Earl Grey?"

"Out of tea for one thing," Corwen shrugged. "And err..." he fished around in the nearest bin and pulled out Gladstone. He'd broken in two.

"I poured the hot water in and..." Luke made a splitting motion with his hands. I grumbled, displeased, and took another sip.

"If I wanted coffee I'd go to that place downstairs," I groused. "At least I wouldn't have to scale the north face of Kilimanjaro every time I wanted a drink."

"You get attacked by jaguars if you do that," Corwen jabbed.

"Jaguars live in Central America," Daisy, who was busy at a computer and appearing to ignore the rest of the room, said.

"Then what about that Hemingway book? The one about the mountaineering expedition who froze to death and then the last survivor got eaten by a jaguar? Read it in school. *The Snows of Kilimanjaro?*"

"Are you *sure* that's the plot?" It had been a long time

since I had read Hemingway but I didn't remember any mountaineering expedition freezing to death.

"Did you find out about this new detective they're sending me?" I asked, turning specifically to Daisy.

As if it wasn't bad enough that I'd been lumbered with a promotion to D.I (without asking for it and refusing the job three times), Cheshire Constabulary were insistent on sending me a sidekick in the form of Detective Sergeant Imogen Gershwin. I was convinced that they were attempting to turn me into some clichéd TV detective and that they'd next be asking me to start drinking and doing maverick things like breaking the rules and beating up suspects and screaming at frightened witnesses in the interview room. They wouldn't even tell me anything about this lady, other than that she was Detective Sergeant Imogen Gershwin. That was why I had gone behind their backs and asked Corwen's lot to see what they could dig up.

"Nothing other than that Imogen Gershwin isn't her full name... Well it is but a few years ago she shortened it by deed poll. Her full name is Imogen Virginia Elaine Gershwin Ophelia Tiffany Abigail Louisa Olive Victoria

Eileen Rebecca Laura Yasmin Blossom Ursula Nadine Colette Hephzibah Oriana Francine Catherine Orchid Clara Offenbach Nelly Una Tabitha Smith."

"Blimey... No wonder she shortened it," Corwen guffawed.

"Too many O's," I said. "If her parents couldn't think of any O names other than Orchid and Offenbach..." Luke handed me the name written down on a piece of paper and I saw immediately why there were too many O's. Her parents must have either been proper jokers or particularly cruel to give her a name like that.

"There's nothing much else to tell. Forty three, stable childhood in Northern Ireland. Place called Crom. Divorced with two children, both girls... Used to be a Detective Inspector but got demoted."

"Why was she demoted?" I didn't want to know that information but felt that I *needed* to know it, especially if I was going to work with her.

"Maverick behaviour," Daisy answered.

All I could think was: 'Oh hell.'

What did they think they were doing by sending me a maverick? Hoping some of it would rub off on me? They really were trying to turn me into a walking cliché.

I, of course, felt that I had to voice this opinion to the rest of the room, though they didn't have much in the way of sympathy. Corwen especially didn't have much sympathy.

"Nah Pops. They'd never be able to do it. What's the crime like around here? Theft and public disorder most of the time. Nearly all of that happens outside Rosie's on a Thursday night. I mean, it's not like…"

My phone began to buzz, as though it took offence to the suggestion that crime in Chester was no more than theft and public disorder on a Thursday night. There *was* more to it than that, but Corwen was right. The city is hardly a hot bed of serious crime. Maybe it isn't the safest place to live in the country, but it's hardly Newport or Worton or downtown Norwich.

"Alright… This better not be another claim about escaped jaguars," I warned.

"Erm…" Baskin, on the other end of the line, fumbled. "We've just had a call, sir…"

"Is it about escaped jaguars? I'm sick to the teeth of them."

"It's not exactly about escaped jaguars but… Well I don't

know… Oh Jesus… Erm…"

"Spit it out man!"

"We've just had a call sir… A dustman has found a body…"

"A body?"

Every ear in the office pricked up.

"It doesn't sound very nice sir… Apparently it's been… Well… I don't know how to say this… It looks like it's been eaten by something, sir."

"Where?"

"Crook Street."

Mere yards from the entrance to this office.

Before Earl Grey could stop sloshing coffee over the desk I was racing through the door and down the stairs, Corwen and Luke behind.

"Where the hell do you two think you're going?" I snatched back at them, half way down.

"We figured you might need help."

"Being nosy more like," I groused, supposing then that I could use them as extra muscle and to keep the gawkers at bay. If this was a jaguar attack then the less people who were hanging around the less there were to spread gossip and panic.

I ran faster than I had since I was plodding the streets of Newport and getting spat on for wearing a uniform. I almost fell down the last few steps into the passageway and the bang as I threw open the insignificant, unnoticed, brown door that led onto the street was enough to alarm the multitude who were flapping around. The sight of Corwen and Luke in hot pursuit, not fast enough to catch up to a man thirty years their senior, made them aware that something was going on and they followed with their eyes and craned their necks to see where we were going.

Unfortunately that was only enough of a sprint to make me lose breath but not nearly enough for people to lose sight of us.

Crook Street is a dirty little alley leading to a dead end, back end part of the city of not much interest that was also called Crook Street. Down there were the backs of some shops and a place for workers to park their cars, a not all that nice social club and a sizeable nest of hideous recruitment consultants.

There was little enough down there that through traffic would be minimal, but not completely null and void. It was still busy enough that, in broad daylight, a jaguar could attack a man and not go unnoticed through his screams.

That was *if* he was attacked in broad daylight. If he was attacked in the dead of night then there was almost no chance of being heard. And few enough people came down here that the body would remain undetected for a while. Most of a morning in fact.

I skidded to a stop in front of a crowd of worried people who were gathered at the entrance to the alley. With them were two uniforms trying to keep order and keep people away from the alley. Outside the tapas bar opposite were two women doing their best to comfort a burly, bald dustman in a reflective jacket, sat on a chair pulled out from the bar. Weeping.

I fumbled for my warrant card and flashed it to the uniforms, one of whom discretely indicated to part way down the alley where there was what looked like a pile of rags and rubbish against the wall. It was innocuous enough that most people would walk past without giving it a second thought.

"These two are with me," I said to the uniforms, indicating Corwen and Luke. "Colman, see if you can get something to cover the view from that row above the tapas bar. I don't want anybody overlooking the crime scene. Corwen, guard these steps into the alley. Make sure nobody comes down them."

Chester's famous rows may be lovely to look at, may be a site of global historic significance, but they can be a nightmare when it comes to sealing off a crime scene. People can look down from above, directly onto the scene, and in some cases you have to seal off the site on more than the usual two or three sides, especially if the crime has occurred in an awkward place like this one had- Not that it happened all that often but it wasn't unknown.

Looking around now I figured that I might need to cordon off a portion of Watergate Street as well, at least as far as the *Age UK* on one end and the toy store on the other. The top of the rows I probably had no need to cordon off so that would mean at least four sets of stairs to seal. Then I would need to block Crook Street on at least two sides.

I would actually need a whole nine lines for this one, as well as sheets to cover up the view from the rows so that we didn't attract an arena of spectators. Lord knows police cordons attract enough of a crowd as it is without having a medieval platform overlooking the scene as well. It's having to seal off such crime scenes that makes me hate Chester sometimes.

I advanced down the alley, knelt down and peeled back the first layer of rag.

Oh Jesus, Mary and Joseph!

It *was* human, I could see as much by the fact that it was wearing the remains of a suit. It was a human that a wild animal had tucked into at some point. No human could have done that. No machine could have done that. There was no doubt in my mind. This was the work of an animal.

I backed back to the light of Watergate Street, wanting to resign and run away to the countryside to one of those villages you see on comedy-dramas where nothing especially serious ever happens and where some resident you've never seen or heard of before (and probably never will again, despite everybody apparently having known them for years) turns up at least once a week. Somewhere I could keep bees!

Steeling myself and doing my best to put the image of what was beneath the rag to the back of my mind, unsuccessfully, I moved towards the weeping dustman. This was a horrible thing I had to do now, as horrible as peering under the rag. He was in no fit state for it but it was my duty as a police officer to do it.

He was a big man. A bruiser with multiple chins. Powerful muscles and three day old stubble. As I approached he was incoherently babbling to the two women and for the first time I noticed an undrunk cup of tea, half the size of his hands, tightly clutched between his stubby, quaking fingers.

"I'm sorry about this," I said to him, tenderly, "but I just need to ask you a few questions."

He nodded and tried to drink from the cup but he was trembling so much the liquid only sloshed down his front.

"It was you who found the body?" He nodded and tried another drink. This time he was more successful. "Can I ask your name?" He tried to get some words out but I couldn't quite get them, they were so mumbled and full of tears.

"His name is Gavin Donegan," one of the women told me.

"Was it you who covered the body Mr Donegan?" he shook his head. "Do you know who did?" He said something that sounded like it was already covered when he found it. I gave him a friendly smile.

"Ok... Somebody will need to take a proper statement from you in a short while, yes?" He nodded and I left him alone to recover, if indeed he ever could.

On my way to the other end of alley I caught Corwen stood at the top of the steps I had ordered him to guard, holding a stance that was similar to a barbarous nightclub bouncer. I ordered him, at the top of my voice, to stand like a normal human being.

Across the street Luke and a step ladder were putting up a dust sheet borrowed from a nearby barber's. It was just about big enough to fill the gap between the columns of the row. He was even doing a half way competent job. He might make a decent police officer if he ever decided to leave the international security business.

At the far end the alley was blocked by Donegan's dust cart. It wasn't one of those big, noisy things with a hydraulic crusher on the back, one which takes five people and an engineering qualification to operate. This was your small, city centre, street patrolling, throw whatever garbage you find in over the top kind of dust cart, an aid for unintrusively keeping the streets clean during daylight hours. It was still large enough to block out the light.

The engine was rumbling away and the door was open so I reached in and turned the key.

I heard someone speaking on the far side of the cart.

"Alright dudes and dudettes…" The way he was speaking sounded weird. It was *really* weird and instantaneously annoying. "I'm gunna see if P.C Freak-out has gone and if he has then we'll sneak a look under that rag! Yaaah? Cool brah… Let's check-ay it out!"

I heard footsteps moving around the dust cart. Staying exactly where I was I waited and watched as a scrawny kid in an expensive looking coat came into my eyeline. He did a side on look down the alley, saw nobody was watching, and then lifted a video camera, pointing it at himself.

"Ok… P.C Freak-out has gone… Let's checky-check-ay this bad bay oooowwwwwt yaaaah?"

What the hell was this idiot doing? Sniffing around a crime scene with a video camera? Did he have any sense? He hadn't yet seen me lurking behind him so as soon as he started advancing down the alley, camera outstretched, I laid hands on him.

"You're nicked sunshine," I proclaimed aloud. He span around and nearly walloped me with the camera. I swung out of the way and lost my grip on his shoulder, just as he shouted: 'Awww shiiii-iiittt... It's P.C Freak-out y'all!' He started to run down the alley, right through my fucking crime scene.

Before I could chase him a well-dressed lady had come down the alley from the other end and had pushed him against the wall with one hand, catching the camera with the other as he dropped it.

"Perhaps you didn't hear the man? He said you're nicked!" By the Irish accent I didn't need to be told that this was my new detective sergeant.

"Awww... What for? I ain't done nutty wrong!"

Gershwin tossed me the camera, reached for her belt and slapped a pair of cuffs on him.

"Try intruding upon a crime scene for a start!" I turned him around so that he was facing us. "Then there's whatever you were trying to do with this..." I waved the camera in his face and then noticed he was wearing a tie, a band of green followed by a band of blue then a thin white line before the pattern repeated. Distinctive. Not hard to work out that he was a pupil at King's.

"I'm sure your headmaster would *love* to hear that you've

been bunking off as well. I know him personally and I also know that he won't be pleased to hear that one of his pupils has been arrested for a serious offence! Now why in the name of God are you here with this thing?"

He didn't look in the least bit remorseful or sorry. He looked proud of himself. His sort are always the worst.

"I'm getting those sweet, sweeeet ay-asss views, ain't I blud?"

"Views?"

"Yah mate... YouTube views."

Oh Christ! An internet fame whore using someone else's suffering for his own gains on top of a potential animal attack. I was already feeling sick but this kid made me feel worse.

"Do I have permission to tear this little gobshite's bollocks off sir?" Gershwin sounded as enraged as I felt sick.

"No sergeant. I've got a better idea. He wants to see what's under the rag... Show him."

Gershwin peeled back the rag, caught a glimpse then refused to look. I remained concentrated on the face of this little rat. He didn't look shocked, alas. He looked excited.

"Awww maaayaaate! Gi me ma cameraaaw mayaaate! This is goooold!"

"Speak like a fucking human being you little gobshite," Gershwin warned.

"Blud this is sick! I gotta film it… Gi me ma cameraaaw back yah?" Gershwin put the rag back down.

"You put that thing there?" I growled. Only now did the kid look shocked.

"What? Nah mate… But this is wicked! This is sick… This is gonna get me, like, ten million views!" He was dancing around like a jackalope. I was tempted to let Gershwin tear his bollocks off. I was tempted to pull his bollocks off myself.

"The only uploading you're going to be doing is being uploaded to a crown court appearance."

Pushed him down the alley to the two uniforms who were keeping the shoppers at bay.

"Have somebody escort him down to the station," I told them. "Stick him in a cell and put this camera down as evidence."

"I know that guy," Luke said as the kid was being led away, shouting about how he was being unfairly treated in that really stupid, annoying way that was somewhere been a chav, a gangsta-rap artist and an imbecile. "He's this really big, really annoying internet celebrity. He goes by the username of Ubi-Hobb-Throb. Really popular with tweenage girls."

"That thing?" I wretched. What was the world coming to if annoying bits of flem like him were what all the tweenage girls were into these days? Justin Beiber and Twilight had been bad enough but at least they had the tenacity to be sane. Now they'd all moved onto that thing? There was no hope. Humanity was doomed.

Gershwin looked Luke up and down and pulled a confused face. Luke definitely wasn't the type to watch annoying internet video stars who are usually fawned over by tweenage girls.

"How do you know this?"

Luke blushed, embarrassed.

"I was keeping an eye on the escaped jaguar situation," he admitted. "Will's orders. I know it's just an overreaction by people on the internet but… Or I thought it was…" He looked nervously at the rags part way down the alley. "This guy came up early on. He's been making videos on the jaguar, stoking people up. Fanning the flames."

"Has he indeed?" I sighed. "Alright... I want you to get whatever notes you have on this twit down to the station and I want a briefing on who this guy is and his connection to the escaped jaguar story." Luke saluted and vanished off down the street, back to his office to collect his notes on this Ubi-Hobb-Throb.

"You think this *is* the escaped jaguar?"

"No. And for one reason... This crime scene." Gershwin scanned the alley.

"Because the attack didn't happen here?" she surmised. "If it had happened here there would be bits of body all over the alley."

"I wasn't referring to that, though it is a good point. No... What I was thinking of was the rag covering the body. That's not the work of an animal. That's human. Somebody put this here. This person was attacked by an animal, I'm sure, but somebody has dumped the remains here after the fact."

"You think it was that little *YouTube* shit?"

"Quite possibly. He could have put this here to freak people out, to fuel his escaped jaguar fantasy. If that's the case though, where did he find someone who had been attacked by a wild animal? Did he do this himself? Did he lure someone into being attacked? If it is we're looking at pre-meditated murder. If it is pre-meditated murder, again, where did he get the wild animal?"

"Could be that he started the whole jaguar rumour himself for views, so he could do this… But that's extreme!"

"It is. There would also be no chance of making sure the story went viral like it did and that would scupper his plan. I do get the feeling he was jumping on a bandwagon."

"He's a kid. Would a kid be twisted enough to do this? Plus, someone like him isn't going to be able to get hold of a jaguar very easily. I doubt most people could."

"Precisely." I knelt down by the rag, pondering. "It's obvious to me why whoever did this dumped this poor sod here. They did it to spread panic, to fan the rumours of an escaped animal roaming the city. That's a motive that fits our video gobshite. But I don't think he'd have the means to do it. As for any other suspects… We'll need to know who this is before we can find them."

"That could lead us back to the little gobshite. This could be his father, his mother… An uncle… A brother…"

"If he fed one of his own relatives to a jaguar for views I swear that I will personally march into YouTube headquarters and shut the site down myself!"

Sirens and wailing police cars. Watergate Street and Crook Street sealed off. The view from the rows impeded. Uniforms going up and down the street asking questions. There was not much that could be done, other than speculate, until Pearson the pathologist and his forensics team arrived. He was not long in coming and, as ever, he did his job with brutal efficiency.

The first thing Gershwin and I knew of his coming was a curly haired presence in the alley kneeling down beside the rag and examining the ground around it.

"Clearly been dumped… Not been here long… The ground looks to be damp underneath from last night's rain… Obviously dumped *after* the rain because the rag is dry."

Pearson fell to silence and contemplated removing the rag. "Do I even want to see this?"

"It isn't nice," Gershwin told.

"How bad?"

"Nothing I ever saw in Newport was as bad as that," I said. Pearson nodded and took hold of the edge of the rag whilst Gershwin and I turned away.

"OH FUCKING BLOODY DELIA SMITH ROASTING HERSELF ALIVE!"

Pearson dropped the rag and sprang back to the other side of the alley.

"You ok?" I asked.

"Do I look ok? That… THAT… That is the worst thing I have ever seen!"

Even Pearson was disturbed by this, and it was his job to look at horrible things. So what did it say about our little gobshite who got all excited over it? Either that he wasn't right in the head or that he already knew what was under there. Or both considering what we were dealing with.

"Definitely an animal attack?"

"*Definitely* an animal attack!"

Pearson reluctantly peeled back the rag once more and gave a 'Delia Smith roasting herself alive,' under his breath. He sat there for a long time, breathing in deeply and trying to examine the corpse without retching. He had more stomach than I did. I wouldn't have been able to do that for all the world.

"On initial examination I'd say this was a male. Perhaps... Maybe mid to late sixties. Some of the bones look to be missing. Whatever did this didn't care what it ate. Flesh, bone. Bits of suit. Teeth look to be in good shape so we should be able to identify him from dental records."

Pearson closed his eyes and breathed deep before taking another look. This time he bent close to the body and prodded it with the end of a pen. Then there was another 'Delia Smith roasting herself alive.'

"What is it?" Gershwin interrogated. Pearson put the rag back and stood up. He stared us both down with a look that said he was not happy.

"D.I Proctor, D.S Gershwin... There is one sick, twisted, perverted little bastard running around this town. A body dumped in an alleyway? Sick enough. A body dumped after being attacked by a wild animal? Even worse. But this takes the proverbial!"

"Do I want to know?"

Pearson was furious in his response.

"No, D.I Proctor… You don't… But this pervert needs to be caught so I'm going to tell you. This man has been dead for at least a week. We're not just looking at someone who was attacked by an animal. You can't even call it an attack! This man has been *fed* to an animal *post mortem*!"

EXHIBIT B: Verpa Vlogarii

"Are we even looking at a jaguar any more?" Gershwin asked as we made our way to the station.

I was enraged. I was more than enraged. I was livid and disturbed and in the mood for smashing things up. I can keep my cool at the most extreme of times but this was testing me to the limits.

"To be honest I don't care," I said. "Whatever it was I don't care... Jaguar, panther, predatory wildebeest... I just want to catch whoever decided it would be fun to feed someone's corpse to an animal before dumping the remains in the city centre."

"The little gobshite?"

"I hope so. It'll give us an excuse to rip his bollocks off and feed them to him! It's looking less and less likely though. Not only would he have had to find a wild animal, but a corpse to feed to it as well."

"Could still be a relative," Gershwin suggested. That was one truly abhorrent thought.

"If he's been feeding his grandfather's corpse to a jaguar for YouTube views then I am going to destroy the internet. If he's going to do shit like that then humanity doesn't deserve it."

Inside the station CID room Luke was waiting to give his presentation and Baskin and Reeves were waiting for orders.

"Sir… We've got the kid in a cell for now," Reeves said as we entered. "He's called his mum and she'll be here in an hour."

"An hour?" If Corwen was in a cell I'd be down to the station right away. I'd leave him in the cell but I'd still get right down to the station.

"Apparently she's having lunch with a friend." There was a long pause. "Sir… He sounded really excited on the phone. Like not sorry at all. He sounded like he was celebrating. Sasha had to warn him that he was in here for a serious offence."

"Does this twit even have any concept of the real world?" I despaired.

"His mother doesn't come across as being much better. What kind of mother doesn't even break off a dinner date when her son has been arrested?"

"Alright, D.S Gershwin. If it was one of your daughters in a cell, what would you do?" I asked.

"Personally? I'd beat the living shit out of them for getting themselves arrested. Whatever I was doing, even if I were on the other side of the world, I'd be there to wallop them as fast as I could get. I don't believe in beating as a form of discipline but getting arrested is an exception."

"You were demoted for maverick behaviour, I believe?" I pointed out, sitting down at my old desk, which now, by rights, belonged to Gershwin. I had been given the small office at the back. Gershwin sat on the chair opposite.

"You've heard of Harresh Kasim, the Silbury gang lord?"

"You mean kebab hand?" Luke jumped in, interrupting, spinning his chair across the room towards us.

"Luke... Please don't call someone kebab hand! If this man has a hook or some kind of implement in place of a hand..."

"That's what they call him," Gershwin said. "He even uses it himself. Though from what I saw he's not got a kebab skewer for a hand like all the rumours say he has."

"Rumours?"

"You haven't heard anything of this guy then?"

"No I haven't!"

"Well all I'll say is that I tried to fit him up and plant evidence to bring him down. My old boss found out and he gave me a choice. Either I accept a demotion and transfer somewhere quiet and out of the way or I could face a full inquiry and damn every other investigation into Kasim's business practices. I made my choice and here I am. Though from what I've seen so far it doesn't seem very quiet."

Whilst I processed this I urged Luke to give his briefing on our gobshite video star. Baskin and Reeves joined us.

The briefing started with a picture, one that wasn't recent because in it the kid looked like he'd only had half a haircut whereas right now his broccoli mop was thick. In the photo he looked the very definition of what the kids these days mistakenly think of as trendy.

"This," Luke pointed to the picture. "Is Ubi-Hobb-Throb- Real name Jessie Hobb- Age fourteen- YouTube star. Twelve million subscribers and almost one billion views in the last year. He uploads a ten minute video every day without fail. He's been circulating the platform for three years but eighteen months ago he hit big.

Luke fiddled with the nearest computer and brought up the video that had made Hobb an internet megastar. It showed Hobb, as he was in the picture, being followed around Connah's Quay with an unseen co-conspirator (operating the camera) and a water blaster, jumping out at random people, soaking them. These people were obviously annoyed and upset, without fail, but Hobb didn't apologise. Every time he just ran away laughing whilst screaming 'it's just a prank braaah… It's just a prank,' in an annoying voice.

All of us, myself, Gershwin, Baskin and Reeves, had some derogatory and unrepeatable comments about this video. One of Hobb's targets was a woman who, when he jumped out, screamed in terror. She started crying when he, unapologetically, drenched her to the bone before running away and screaming his catchphrase of 'it's just a prank braaah!'

"Who was his camera man?" Gershwin asked. She was making notes of her own. On the page I could see she had written the title of the video and: '*evidence of assault*?'

"No idea… But a huge proportion of his videos are like

this. He never uses one particular place for what he calls his 'pranks' but they're all somewhere within easy reach of Chester… Connah's Quay, Parkgate, Flint, Wrecsam, Ellesmere Port."

"How extreme are these so called pranks?"

"Most of them involve assaulting pedestrians in some way. Jumping out at them with water blasters. He *loves* that one. There's one where he screams in people's ear which is particularly…"

Luke brought it up on screen. This was far worse than the water blaster video, far worse. I don't even want to recall it. It made my blood froth.

"Has he ever done anything physically violent? Has he ever shown any tendency towards doing anything that comes close to what we're looking at?"

"Dumping a mutilated body in an alley? No. Nothing at all. Most of his videos amount to nuisance behaviour bordering on assault or talking rubbish in that stupid voice with lots of screaming.

"About a week ago, when the jaguar photo started to go viral, he began to focus on that. He wasn't the first but he's been one of the loudest voices. Three of his last seven videos have been him shouting about how the jaguar is real and how we're all going to die. The other four... This was from two days ago."

Luke looked positively grim as he clicked through onto another video.

It started with Hobb, hiding behind a wall, giggling and saying that this was going to be his 'bestest prank evaaah braah!' He again had his camera man with him. Hobb pulled a hood over his head and a mask over his face. Then jumped he from behind the wall and started creeping towards... I gritted my teeth and my fingers clenched around the arm of the chair... A Jaguar car dealership!

'Are there any Jaguar dealerships nearby?' I asked aloud. I didn't know of any and this definitely didn't look like Chester. Luke paused the video.

"I checked and the answer is no... But I found where this was from the sign here in the background. The one that says *Chung Ku Restaurant*. It's Liverpool. Just outside Toxteth."

"Dangerous place to be making prank videos," I grimaced. "And who thought of opening a Jaguar dealership in Toxteth? That's like rubbing salt into a wound."

Luke restarted the video and Hobb, followed by his cameraman, snuck up to one of the cars and hid behind it. Then from his bag he pulled out a can of spray paint and painted the words 'escaped' all over it before giggling, as if it were funny. Then, unseen, they ran up to the dealership itself and started spray painting on the window.

Hobb had got to the P of *escaped* when one of the salesmen caught him. There was a scream, a shout, and then Hobb and the cameraman running from the scene with the salesman giving chase. Gershwin added '*mindless vandalism, Jaguar, Toxteth… Confirmed*,' to her notes.

On screen there was a change, an edit. It was clearly some time later because it had grown darker and Hobb was wearing different clothes.

"Alright D-cup braah's… Part one was wicky wickad so now let's move onto part twoooo yaaaah?" He again went off towards the Jaguar dealership, but this time bold as brass. There were uniforms there, I could see, examining the window which Hobb had earlier graffitied. He turned excitedly to his camera man.

"Awww sweee-et brah! The po-po have come sniffing round! We can 'ave even more fun wid dis one!"

He continued striding towards the dealership and right up to a salesman who was checking every car for signs of damage. He was a fair distance from the uniforms.

"Scusey me may-at... Have any of your Jag-wahs been chompin down on people?"

"I beg your pardon?" the salesman, an obvious scouser, was understandably confused.

"Chompin down on people... Going for munchies... Eating them..."

"Piss off kid," the salesman snapped, having no time for such stupid inanities.

"I think they 'ave braah... One of them chased me and mah mate Spicksey down the street... Its lid were doing all this..." He made an alligator snapping motion with his hand.

"Turn it off!" I ordered. "That's enough. We get the picture. And that's all he's been doing?" Luke nodded.

"Seems like it." I stood up and started pacing.

"Right... I want to know why this idiot was sniffing around my crime scene. How did he know there was an animal attack there? Is there any chance *at all* that he planted the body? He's got motive. This could be one of his pranks, brah. I want someone to check his camera footage. Volunteers?"

"I will," Gershwin raised her hand.

"Excellent… Baskin? I want you to go through all his so called prank videos. You recorded the places, Luke?"

"It took some work, but yeah. Got them all down."

"Excellent. Baskin. Look through the videos and cross reference the locations with any reports involving the specific 'prank' in the days leading up to the upload. Reeves. See if you can find me a wild predator expert. I want to know what we might be dealing with. Jaguar, predatory wildebeest or whatever. I want to know where on earth this thing might have come from. Is there any way the would be Jeremy Beadle could have got hold of such an animal? If not him, then who could?"

"Sir," Baskin raised his hand. "Are any questions going to be asked if this kid's bollocks mysteriously disappear?"

"None whatsoever!"

I moved into my office, agitated and in need of a good scream. I sank down behind my desk and buried my head in my knees. This was turning into the day from hell.

It was about to get worse.

Pearson flounced in.

"I'm going to resign," he declared.

"You can't. You're the best pathologist in the county."

"After today I don't want to be a pathologist any more."

I pushed Hobb's photo at him.

"Right now this kid is prime suspect number one." Pearson grimaced at the photo.

"Jessie Hobb… I know him. I had to ban my daughter from watching his videos. Twisted little freak! I don't think he could have done it."

"Why not?"

"I've just had the remains transferred up to Blacon. There's no way Hobb could have transferred them to Crook Street so cleanly. He'd need a vehicle. Not only that, the remains would have been too heavy for a weedy fourteen year old kid like him to lift on his own."

"So he had help," I shrugged. "He has a co-conspirator for some of his videos. A cameraman…"

"He'd also have had to either break into a funeral parlour or go grave robbing," Pearson said. "I've not confirmed this with tests, but I think the body has been professionally prepared for burial or cremation. Either way, that corpse has been through the system at some stage."

I couldn't believe I was hearing this. This was something out of a nightmare which kept getting more and more ludicrous.

"Right… So what are the chances? Bollox rumours of an escaped jaguar… Fine… Conspiracy nutters come out with this crap all the time… But then all this with the body. With it being dumped, not attacked at the scene. Then with it being dead to begin with. Now you're telling me whoever this person is they've been *body snatched*? Why would anyone do all this? If it was to make people panic they could have just dumped a load of butcher's meat in the alley. Arranged it to look like an attack. Nobody would go to the trouble of actually snatching a body, feeding it to an animal and *then* dumping it just to make people panic."

"Even for a prank video it's over the top," Pearson grieved. "Even in that context it's extreme."

"There is one possibility," I regretted. "We could be looking at a maniac. Not homicidal. If this person were homicidal then he wouldn't have bothered snatching a corpse."

"I suppose Hobb might fit that profile," Pearson

suggested. "But I still don't think he could have done it without a vehicle."

"When do you suppose the body was left there?"

"Had to be some time last night. I'd suggest late, when there was nobody around."

"If whoever did this used a vehicle then it would have been caught on camera. I'll have Reeves check through last night's footage once he's done finding me a wild predator expert."

There was a knock on the door, Gershwin carrying a laptop.

"Sir... I've checked the camera and it suggests Hobb was acting on a tip off from someone." She put the laptop down on my desk and brought a folder up. "There are three video files on the camera card, all from this morning. Two are the usual bollox, him sneaking around the crime scene till he gets caught. One of them has you looking at the body, sir. He seems to find it hilarious. The first is the most interesting though." Gershwin let the first file on the card play.

It was rougher than the uploaded stuff, lots more pauses and faffing about trying to get his angles right, but Hobb was still the same annoying little shit as ever.

"Alright d-cup braahs..." He used that one in an earlier video and it was just as cringey then. "Some old gezzer on twittah-twit hooked me up wid a source. Said I needed to get down to Crook Street coz there's evidence of our jaggy down dere. I don't know if he telling the tooth or not but if he ain't ima gunna find him and beat his dentures owwwt. Know wad I'm-ah sayin' braaahs?" Hobb made some sort of weird gesture with his hands.

"See. Threatening people!" Pearson pointed. "If Corwen was a ten year old girl would you let him watch that?"

"If Corwen was a ten year old girl then my life would be a lot simpler!"

"I sincerely hope my daughters aren't watching this shit-bag. If they are there'll be hell to pay," Gershwin snorted.

We watched the rest of this clip. It was mainly Hobb being a nuisance on the rows, the side opposite to Crook Street, until he reached the barber's, where he swung the camera round. The two uniforms who had been there when I had arrived were talking to people, trying to keep them back. There was a buzz going on around the place. Hobb turned the camera back on himself.

"Awww shiiit braahs. Looks like the po-po have got here first... But what's that down there?" He turned the camera back around and zoomed in on the rags which covered the remains. "That looks like sometin. Let's sneak round da back and get a looksies for ourself, yah?"

There the clip ended.

"Have you checked the tweet?" I asked Gershwin as she closed the laptop.

"Yes sir. It seems genuine. His timeline shows a retweet from Gordon Gloucester, posted to him at around seven this morning and retweeted just before nine. It says..." She checked her notes. "Hey kid... Get yourself down to Crook Street, Chester. Massive jaguar evidence!"

"And Hobb just took that?"

"I had a look at Gloucester's twitter feed. He doesn't look like the type to dupe children, even irritating ones."

"Who is he?"

"Local man by the looks of it. Animal lover. Tweets a lot of RSPCA animal charity stuff. He also seems to have a close connection with St Blaise's church in Christleton."

"ST BLAISE'S!" Pearson and I chorused together.

"Is that significant?"

"St Blaise's," Pearson said, "Is where the photo that first started the whole jaguar rumour was taken."

"This case gets stranger and stranger," I said. "Putting aside the St Blaise's connection for the moment, what does Gloucester want with a fourteen year old internet star? Assuming, for a moment, based on that tweet, that it was Gloucester who dumped the body, why would he then want to lure some kid to the remains?"

"Could be a coincidence," Pearson suggested. Gershwin and I both simultaneously shook our heads. It was not a coincidence.

"Gloucester definitely doesn't look the type to watch internet videos, especially not ones like Hobb's. Reading through his tweets he seems... Kind... Genial... He seems like the kind of man who would side with the victims rather than the perpetrator."

"Something about all this doesn't add up," I groused for about the thousandth time that day.

"We don't have all the evidence yet," Gershwin said, side eying Pearson and hinting that he should get on with identifying the corpse. He took the hint and threw it back at her.

"Yes… Well… I'm procrastinating… I'm thinking that if I sit here long enough I'll reach retirement age and somebody else will have to identify the poor sucker." Gershwin and I glared at him and he gave up.

Yes, it was horrible, but his job was to look at horrible things. This one just happened to be more horrible than most.

"Fine… But don't ever ask me to identify any corpse ever again… Next time you can do it yourself!"

"Next time it's likely to be some old dear in Handbridge who's passed away in her sleep aged one hundred and two."

"Oh if only this were, if only this were," Pearson lamented as he passed out of the office.

Reeves' head replaced him.

"Sir. I've got you a wild predator expert. Doctor Caroline Faulkner, lecturer in animal studies at the university. Specialises in South and Central American mammals."

"Jaguars?"

"Jaguars!" I grinned for the first time since the body had been discovered.

"One problem. She's currently flying back from a conference in Brazil and won't land until eight tomorrow morning."

"Then we'll pay her a visit first thing. Can you leave a message for her? Excellent!"

"One more thing, there's a man in reception claiming to be Andrew Parsons, Jessie Hobb's father."

"Even better. Maybe we can persuade him to exert some influence over his errant son."

"If he hasn't already, there's no hope," Gershwin corrected. A fair point.

"Perhaps. But if there is no hope then I'll make sure he regrets it for the rest of his days."

"That sounds like you plan on indulging in some maverick behaviour!"

"There are more ways of making someone regret something than with maverick behaviour, Sergeant Gershwin. Like making him feel the guilt of his son's actions, for example?"

I walked out into the main office.

"Reeves, I want you to check all the CCTV in and out of Crook Street and Watergate Street for last night between half nine and seven this morning. I want the plate of every car that went through and the name of every driver. I want you to keep an eye out for one name in particular, Gordon Gloucester."

"Gordon Gloucester. Got it chief!"

Andrew Parsons was a drip from the Black Country. He was a coward who looked uncomfortable in his own skin. A weed with a pathetic drone of a brummie accent. Gershwin dealt with him initially, whilst he sat in the reception in his padded blue overcoat and tried to come up with lame excuses for his son.

"He doesn't mean to cause any harm… Do you Jess?" he said after we had sat him down in the interview room and showed him the water blaster video. 'Jess' shook his head. He'd suddenly lost his tongue. "He's only having a bit of fun… It's…"

"It's what? Just a prank, brah?" From the look in Parson's eyes he really didn't like D.S Gershwin. She didn't much like him either.

I was on her side. It was no wonder Hobb was so out of control, pathetic and off the leash. His father couldn't have exerted influence over a wet paper bag. His mother, who had decided not to cut short her dinner date after all, obviously didn't care.

I threw a video still at him to see if that would change his mind.

"That lady there was clearly distressed. The video shows her in tears… IN… TEARS!"

Parsons' lip quivered.

"I'm sure it was just the shock," he tried to excuse.

Gershwin and I were keeping a stress toy under the desk and passing it between us. It was getting rough treatment as Hobb and his father were pushing us both to our limits. I, who currently had hold of it, clamped down and turned to Hobb.

"And what do you think, Jeremy Beadle? Was it just the shock?" He looked confused over 'Jeremy Beadle' but then the rest of my question worked its way into the swamp.

"Yah blud… It were just the shock!"

"You made a lady cry. Do you not think that was wrong?"

"Nah blud. She got over it!"

"And what if she didn't?" Gershwin asked. I passed her the stress toy. "Do you even know that lady? Do you know what goes through her head? What she's been through? She could be the loneliest woman in the world just wanting somebody to come and give her a hug."

"If she wants a hug she should get herself a boyfriend then." I heard the stress toy begin choking under the desk.

"You are looking at some serious offences young man. Right now one of my DCs is cross checking the dates of all your prank videos with any reports made. If one of them comes back then you are looking at a serious punishment. That's before we add in the fact that we *already have evidence* of assault *and* vandalism, both of which are going to net you serious consequences of their own."

"Evidence?" Parsons looked at us, bemused. "You've not got any evidence!" The stress toy came into my hand. Gershwin had well mangled it during that last question.

"What the hell do you call those videos which show your son 'pranking' people? There's no denying it's him, Mr Parsons."

"I'm sure if we looked at the IP we'd find they were uploaded from your son's computer."

Both Hobb and Parsons were quiet. The stress toy got a moment's recovery.

I took out a picture of Gordon Gloucester and handed it over. Hobb didn't show any sign of recognition.

"That's the man who tweeted you this morning. Ever seen him before?" Hobb shook his head. "Do you have any idea why he might want to lure you to a crime scene?"

"Hang on… *Lure* him to a crime scene?"

"Yes, Mr Parsons. *Lure* him to a crime scene! I doubt that this man is a regular viewer of your son's videos."

Parsons began to splutter and cough before turning towards Hobb.

"What the hell have you done to this man Jess?"

"Ah dunno blud. I ain't never seen this old geeze-pot before in mah life 'ave ah?"

"Please teach your son to speak English, Mr Parsons," Gershwin said. The stress toy was passed over.

"So you've never heard of this man before this morning? Gordon Gloucester. Answer in clear English, please."

"Nah mate. I ain't."

"I said English, Mr Hobb." Hobb tried to stare me down. "I bet your teachers at the King's school don't let you talk like that, do they? DO THEY?" The stress toy came back to me.

"No sir, they don't," Hobb sulked, finally reverting to a normal mode of talking.

"Excellent… Now… Yes or no… Had you ever heard of Gordon Gloucester before he tweeted you this morning.

"No sir, I hadn't."

"What about St Blaise's church?"

"Yah mean where the jaggy jag were spotted?" A stern raised eyebrow, a clench of the stress toy. "I mean… Errr… Where the jaguar was spotted? No. I've never been there." Parsons looked confused. Both Gershwin and I noticed.

"I think you're lying, Mr Hobb," Gershwin said, taking back the stress toy. "Judging by your YouTube channel you've become obsessed with this escaped jaguar story. Why wouldn't you visit St Blaise's, see where it all started? Attempt to track down the jaguar? It would have been more worthwhile than vandalising a car dealership."

"What? I didn't do that," Hobb protested.

"WE HAVE THE FOOTAGE!!!!" The stress toy went flying across the room, right over the cowering Hobb's head, and collided with the wall.

"For the benefit of the tape, D.S Gershwin has just thrown a stress toy across the room," I said calmly before returning to the matter at hand. Parsons quaveringly collected the toy from the floor and passed it back to Gershwin.

"If you'd never heard of Gordon Gloucester then why did you follow his advice to go to Crook Street this morning?" There was no answer. "Some random stranger tweets you and you go? That doesn't sound like sensible behaviour to me."

"He looked honest," Hobb said. "Old gezzers like that don't lie, do they?"

"Trust me, they do. I've worked as a police officer for long enough to know that they really do!" Hobb looked ashamed, guilty.

"And when you get there? You see the police. Instead of being sensible you attempt to sneak around them and see what was in the alley."

"I didn't know it was a crime scene did I?"

"What did you *think* the police were doing there? You must have known it was a police matter because you saw my colleague investigating the body. You laughed at him and called him P.C Freak-Out." Parsons laughed but I shot him down with a glare.

"And then after that, even though you had seen my

reaction, you still decided to have a look for yourself. You knowingly attempted to trespass on a crime scene and put your grubby fingers all over evidence."

"You did it!"

"I'm a police officer. I know what the hell I'm doing. You are a child who assaults people for internet views. You even said it yourself when we caught you. What was it he said D.S Gershwin?"

"He said... I'm getting those sweet, sweeeet ay-asss views, ain't I blud?"

"You'd film a corpse for views? Someone who has suffered and who has had their body dumped in an alleyway?"

"He didn't do that," Parsons protested. "How could he have done that when he only found out about it this morning?"

"Maybe he didn't dump the body, Mr Parsons, but *somebody* did. Somebody fed that man to an animal and dumped the leftovers in an alleyway and your son was going to use his corpse for views. Does that not strike you as wrong?"

Parsons couldn't answer. He was looking almost as guilty

as Hobb.

"Mr Parsons, have you *ever* attempted to teach your son a single ounce of decency? The difference between right and wrong? Did you never tell him not to hit other children? Not to take what didn't belong to him? Did you ever teach him to share? To show respect for other people? No. I didn't think so. I'll bet you haven't even had words over these sickening acts he's been uploading to the internet."

"They're just pranks, brah!"

"They're not *just* pranks, brah. This is harming other people. This is being a little bully. This is being a menace to society. A prank is nothing more than a harmless jape, something the other person might find amusing. It is *not* making grown women cry."

I turned back to Parsons.

"This, Mr Parsons, is on you. Your son and his behaviour are *your* responsibility. Your job is to make sure he grows up good and decent and proper. Your job is to stop him from going around assaulting people. You, Mr Parsons, have failed. You have failed both as a father and as a human being. Do you want to know what the cost of that is? Your son will now have a criminal record, a large and serious one. He won't go to university, he'll go to prison, to a young offender's institute. For the rest of his life he will live with the consequences of these so called pranks hanging over his head. And why? Because *you* couldn't teach him some basic respect. Because *you* are a failure!"

I said all this as calmly as I could, though still with a degree of harshness.

I had told Gershwin that were ways besides maverick behaviour to make Parsons feel guilty, and this little speech had done the trick. The guilt of his failures crushed him and he broke down in tears.

We suspended the interview, allowed him time to recover, and returned Hobb to a cell.

There was bad news in the main office.

"I've checked the CCTV footage sir," Reeves admitted. "There were seventeen cars that went down Watergate Street last night and not one of those stopped outside the alley. Those that did stop? No dice. They didn't stop anywhere near Crook Street."

"What about on Crook Street itself?"

"Nothing sir…"

"What?"

"Absolutely nothing between half nine and seven, like you asked for. There were a few pedestrians but none that looked to be carrying a body."

"See if you can identify them. They may be potential witnesses."

My phone rang… Pearson.

"This had better be good news!" I walked over to where Gershwin was setting up an incident board. Pictures of Hobb, of the crime scene, of Gordon Gloucester at a barbecue, the original jaguar image…

"There really isn't much to identify this poor sod," Pearson decried. "The face is chewed to pieces but hopefully we'll still be able to get those dental records."

"Did you find *anything*?"

"Yes… It might help… There's a tattoo on his arm…" All of a sudden my eyes snapped to one of the photos on the board.

"It isn't a lion is it? Left arm, just above the elbow?"

"How in the name of Delia Smith roasting herself alive

did you guess that?"

Because I could see it, clear as day. It was right there in that photo of Gordon Gloucester, right there on his left arm just above the elbow, the tattoo of a lion!

EXHIBIT C: Conochaetes Praedonius

It had all been a dream, a nightmare. Everything from that phone call about the rogue jaguar to the Gladstone mug being broken to the late Gordon Gloucester's tweet luring an annoying internet star to his own mutilated remains. None of it was real. Gordon Gloucester didn't exist and neither did Jessie Hobb. Jessie Hobb couldn't exist. Nobody could be that annoying. The only thing it could all have been was a feverish nightmare.

I lay in bed, seven of the AM, wondering what lovely, simple, uncomplicated nuisances the day would have in store for me. A shoplifter perhaps. An old lady accidentally knocking over a cyclist. A man who'd chopped his own toes off whilst drunk in charge of a lawnmower. That was what I wanted out of today. Nothing that involved bloody corpses or liars or anything more serious than some scuffed elbows and a few missing toes. I wanted simple. I wanted day to day police work. The kind of work that comes in a city where little exciting ever happens. A city where people just get on with their lives and the only thing that ever disturbs me is bloody minded stupidity and incompetence.

I had a blissful shower, warm and soapy and free from the worries of the world.

Then I walked into the kitchen and found the notes I had brought home the night before. Notes on Gordon Gloucester and his demise.

He was sixty seven. Retired naval man. Lived alone in a house on Deans Way, out in Tarvin- A typical, middle class, suburban home of the early eighties with large front garden, garage, plenty of room to potter around in, nosy neighbours. Never married by the looks of it. No children that anyone knew of. No dependencies either. Gloucester was a man who had almost nobody in his life.

He had a twitter account but only six followers, one of which was the official account for St Blaise's church, where he spent a lot of his spare time- One of his last tweets was a photograph of a bat box he'd put up around the back of the churchyard there. One of his other followers was the reverend, Greensborough Dewdrop, whom I unfortunately knew of old. The third was Dewdrop's son, Timothy, the fourth Cheshire Wildlife Trust, and the final two looked to be spam-bots.

In all, his looked like a lonely existence and it was no wonder, therefore, that he had dedicated his life to animals. He was a patron of the zoo, regularly gave to wildlife sanctuaries and charities and bred hedgehogs in his back yard. I would have hazarded a guess that he preferred animals to people. In today's society, where out of control gobshites can run around causing mischief for internet views and get away with it, who wouldn't? Animals don't intentionally hurt you and run away shouting 'it's just a prank brah…'

Ok, wasps… But they're wasps and total bastards anyway.

His death, a week ago, had been exceptionally sad and untimely. Not a natural death, but one of those misfortunes that befalls people from time to time. According to the coroner's report he'd died of carbon monoxide poisoning. The result of an ancient and faulty boiler that hadn't been replaced since the house was built. One of the flues had become clogged and the contraption started leaking poisonous gas. Sat in his armchair, unaware of the toxic air he was breathing, Gloucester slipped away, first into a sleep and then into death. It was painless, he wasn't even aware of it, but that didn't make it any less sad. He'd been discovered the next day by Dewdrop the Elder.

The notes ended with a short paragraph saying that he had been buried in St Blaise's churchyard the day before he was dumped in that alley.

Everything came back to St Blaise's.

The rumour of the escaped jaguar had started there. Gordon Gloucester had attended the church there, spent his time there. The reverend of the church had discovered his body. What the connection was with the heartless thing that had been done to Gloucester's remains I did not yet know, nor of the connection with the would be Jeremy Beadle, but in going there I would find the answer.

I heard the front door open and close again. Corwen? Corwen…

I heard his key drop onto the side table. He'd probably come home to change and scrounge breakfast before going to work. He often did that when he stayed at Carla's. Usually he'd slip his ugly mug around the kitchen door to see what I was up to but today was an exception. I heard his footsteps enter the living room and then nothing. He didn't even switch the television or the radio on like he normally did.

Sensing that something was up I left the notes on the table and went to check on him. He was perched on the sofa, knees up to his chest, vacant, listless stare on his face.

"Corwen? You alright?"

"Huh? Yeah… Fine."

No. He wasn't.

"Has something happened? Between you and Carla?" No answer, just the vacant stare.

Something had happened.

"You can't fool me you know. I didn't get to Detective Inspector without knowing how to weed the truth out of people."

Still no answer. I passed a hand in front of his face, clicked a few times. The vacant expression didn't budge.

I retreated into the kitchen. If Corwen wouldn't answer me then maybe Carla would. I rang her on my mobile and before I had opened my mouth I got an earful.

"If he's getting you to do his begging for him, think again. Don't bother." She hung off. She sounded angry. She sounded enraged. She sounded hysterical. I was left to wonder what the hell was wrong, to contemplate and come up with the solution that Corwen had said something stupid and refused to apologise. That didn't explain his catatonic state. It couldn't just have been that he'd said something stupid. It had to be more serious.

Half an hour later, as I was reading the newspaper, there was a knock on the door. I had quite forgotten that I'd agreed to drive Gershwin down to see this Doctor Caroline Faulkner. I opened the door to see her waving and blowing kisses at a white Volkswagen, quite the opposite character to the rough, bollocks chomping detective sergeant I had worked with the day before.

"My mammy," she explained. "She agreed to drop me off here and take the kids to school. It was easier that way."

"You all live together?"

"Aye. Mammy doesn't have to live alone and I've got somebody to help look after the girls."

"So long as she isn't anything like my mother. I'd rather *not* have a crotchety old scouse madam pottering about the place."

"Ah… You're a man… Men prefer to fly the coop and get away from their mothers as fast as possible. Unless they're chimps or psychopaths. Though, saying that…" She pointed to the still catatonic Corwen, who hadn't noticed the new arrival.

"Oh… His mother and I are divorced. Have been for a long time. Getting on for seventeen years now. Thank goodness."

"Total bitch?"

"Fag hag Audrey Hepburn!"

"Sorry I asked. What's up with him anyway?"

"Not a clue. Some sort of girlfriend trouble I think."

"Speaking of trouble…" Gershwin's face changed from cheery and amiable, the face of a lovely lady, to that of a hardass bitch, the face of the woman I had worked with yesterday.

Gershwin rifled around in the bag which she had with her and pulled out a tablet. Instantly I knew what this would be. Our would be Jeremy Beadle had done something silly. I led Gershwin into the kitchen.

"What has he done now?"

"You remember in the interview yesterday where he said he'd never been to St Blaise's?"

"He lied? Of course he lied. The little gobshite couldn't

tell the truth if you asked him to."

"Worse than that. After he was released on bail last night he uploaded *another* video, in total breach of his bail conditions."

A little voice inside my head told me to scream, to go mad, to stab a cushion with a kitchen knife, to smash a wine bottle or a window. Another part of me was tempted to raid the Christmas sherry and down the lot. I reined myself in, tried to remain calm.

"Right. Let's see it then! It might give us more evidence to throw at him."

"It does that alright," Gershwin smiled sinisterly.

The video was another of those which I absolutely do not want to recall or describe, though I fear that I will have to.

It might well have been Hobb's most disgusting video yet.

The first thing I noticed was the location. Clear as day, that was St Blaise's church. I recognised the steeple and the tower and the old lich gate which some muppet had built a wall through the middle of. There beside it all, was Hobb, claiming to be seeking his 'jaggy-jag.' He was again with his cameraman.

"We need to find out who's been filming these."

"I set Baskin onto it for homework sir. I had him search through Hobb's social media profiles, to see what he could dig up. So far all he's come up with is a nickname. Icepicks."

"Good lass. Hopefully this Icepicks is more sensible than..."

We were still watching the video and I froze as Hobb scooped up something from off the church footpath. It looked like...

Oh, what foul demons created this monstrosity to torment the honest souls of planet earth? What devil walked amongst us in human form? What did we mere mortals do to deserve such damnation?

It looked like, and surely was, a steaming pile of turd.

"Awww... Looky look at this may-ats! Jaggy-jag poop!" Hobb whooped for joy and then started sniffing at the faeces in his hand. He nearly licked it but instead started laughing and ran to the church door and started smearing the poo all over it.

"I don't want to see any more of this," I said, almost vomiting.

"You might want to sir. It... Well..." She pointed to the

notes on Gordon Gloucester, specifically the page which listed his twitter followers.

Thirty seconds later whilst Hobb was prancing about the churchyard with yet more poo, which he'd discovered behind a gravestone, there came onto the scene Timothy Dewdrop- A boy only a year or so older than Hobb. Bookish. Bespectacled. The sort of nice boy all girls avoid with all the desperation of doomsday. Preferring instead the raving lunatic with the poo in his hand.

It looked like Timothy Dewdrop was troubled by something. His eyes were bright red, his clothes (a waistcoat and bowtie) messed up. There was something severely unconfident about him.

"Excuse me," he squeaked at Hobb. "What do you think you're doing?" In the background somebody, also messed up and shaken, holding a smouldering cigarette in one hand, was seen coming around the corner of the church. I recognised him as the Reverend Dewdrop, an especially odious sort of holier-than-thou snob who, based upon only the slightest glimpse, had not changed one bit in the six years since our previous encounter.

Hobb appeared not to notice him.

In response to Dewdrop the Younger's question, Hobb reacted with villainy. He snickered to himself, gurned for the camera, picked up the largest turd he could, and flung it at Dewdrop the Younger. As it hit him Dewdrop the Younger screamed, at which point Hobb pelted him with another turd.

Only now did he see Dewdrop the Elder bearing down on him, dropping his lit cigarette into the grass, grabbing him by the collar and shaking him.

"Geeert off me brah… It's just a prank brah… It's just a prank brah," Hobb screamed before kicking Dewdrop the Elder in the shin. Was that kick just a prank as well? I think not.

All the time something was going on with the camera man. He was backing away although he still held Hobb captive in his viewfinder.

Then Hobb did something unforgivable, even for the cameraman. Freed from Dewdrop the Elder's grip, he picked up another turd, the biggest and sloppiest he could set his hands on, and then…

Dear God. I do not want to repeat it but you might well be able to guess what the disgusting little gobshite did. The camera dropped into the grass and there was a scuffle between two pairs of legs, one pair the cameraman and the other Hobb, before the video ended. No sign off, no explanation.

"Classic sign of doing something for attention that," Gershwin pointed out. "End suddenly. Keep 'em guessing what is going on, that way they'll come back for more, hoping for an explanation."

"I'm more interested in the Reverend Dewdrop to tell you the honest to God truth. I've had a run in with him before. I don't know if he still does, but he used to take RE up at Christleton High, not far from the church." I stood and entered the lounge, hoping I might be able to spur my son into some life by way of unwelcome nostalgia.

"Corwen... You remember the Reverend Dewdrop?" There was no response. "Didn't he call you a godless sinner?" Gershwin put a hand to her mouth and giggled. "No... It wasn't funny."

I couldn't help half smiling for Corwen's face had finally altered. That meant his catatonic state *had* to be related to something Dewdrop had once said to him. To Corwen being a godless sinner. There was only one thing it could be. Only one sin that could make Corwen catatonic.

"What did he say? That you'd get some poor girl pregnant one of these days? Do you think I should tell him that his prophecy has come true?" Corwen's head almost did a one hundred and eighty and his eyes popped out of their sockets.

"How the bloody hell did you guess that?"

"Nearly thirty five years interviewing criminal scum, laddy! You can't pull the wool over the eyes of an old copper!"

"I don't want it," Corwen jabbered. "She insists on keeping it… Saying she can't take a life and all that bullshit… But I don't want it…"

"You tried to beg her to get rid of it?" Corwen nodded. "At the end of the day it's her choice mate. Remember though you *do* have a say in this as well. It's your life we're talking about as well as hers. The two of you need to reach a compromise. Even if you put it up for adoption or foster it out. Think about it… Calm down, have a shower, take a nap… Do whatever… But make sure at some point today you get back round there and sort things out."

"I'll do what Mam did. I'll run off to Rome and live out a

film star fantasy!"

"Become a trampy Richard Burton? That's the coward's way out. Remember as well, the aforementioned mam is going to have kittens when she finds out about this. Your grandmother may also drown you in the nearest river. I'll speak to you later. D.S Gershwin, shall we go and see what we can find out about predatory mammals?"

It was only when we were sat in the car and Gerswhin was figuring out how the seatbelt worked that it actually, properly hit me. I let out an enormous 'Oh Crap!' and gripped the steering wheel so hard that my knuckles turned white.

"Not a fan of this baby then?" Gershwin half grinned.

"No... Actually... No! Do I look old enough to be a grandfather? I don't suppose I would mind if it weren't for *her*!"

"Not a fan of the girlfriend either?"

"She's nice enough but not the kind of person you'd want for a daughter-in-law. And they've only been dating for six months... Worse than that... I keep getting the impression that Corwen has got himself caught up in a rebound and I'm the one who put her last boyfriend behind bars."

"Did she know this when she started dating Corwen?"

"No. It might be a worse situation if she had."

I started the engine and tried to forget about it.

The stereo cut in and started blasting out *Gotta Get a Message to You* by the Bee Gees. Gershwin looked unimpressed so I told her she could pick another CD from the slip case in the glove box. She tutted over the ridiculous number of Bee Gees CDs in there. She didn't look impressed by most of my music collection actually- Bee Gees, Billy Joel, Donna Summer, all those golden greats of the late seventies whom musicians ever since have never topped. I was used to that look of disdain. Corwen hated my music collection in exactly the same way. That was why, at the back, there were a few CDs for his benefit, mainly soul singers of the eighties and mid-nineties.

Gershwin found Whitney Houston and she came over all nostalgic.

"Oh my gosh… My first boyfriend bought me this album! He was a total tit, but I *love* the album!"

In the CD player it went and for the next twenty minutes, until we reached the village of Bruera, where Doctor Faulkner lived, we jammed and sang along to Whitney. It must have been a weird sight- Two middle aged coppers driving along in a third rate (other people's opinion, not mine) sports car blasting out Whitney Houston and joining in with all the songs. At one point, in the mirror, when we were stopped at a set of traffic lights, a lady in a Toyota directly behind was staring in disbelief at the crazy scene before her eyes. Gershwin and I cared not, for we enjoyed ourselves. It took our mind off the lunacy of this case, the stupidity and the sickening behaviour of Jessie Hobb, and the grandchild shaped meteor that had appeared in the skies over my life.

You need that kind of thing when you work in policing. More than any other career you need something to take your mind from the job, to take you elsewhere. Even in a quiet place like Chester we spend our lives wading through the black swamps of human nature. We see so much shit, figurative and literal, every day, so much that is wasted and so much gone awry. So much time is spent attempting to keep the civilised world in order, playing the fiddle which calls the criminal to justice and brings comfort to the befallen. if we didn't distract ourselves we would fall into a desperate abyss. Being silly and singing to Whitney

Houston may only have been a small thing but for that day it would provide a small contribution towards keeping despair at bay for both myself and for Gershwin.

"We should do that again," Gershwin grinned as we climbed out of the car at Doctor Faulkner's house. "Though I'm buying you some better music."

And there our twenty minutes of escapism ended. Now it was time to return to the deadly serious matter of the crime that had been put before us.

Bruera is unforgivably tiny. a village of no more than ten houses, most of them belonging to farms. There is no post office, no pub or inn, not even a little shop for when you need those bare necessities that aren't worth driving all the way to the supermarket for. It was not even what you might call close to the city. Twenty minutes and ten kilometres from my own house in Boughton, which in itself is right on the edge of the Chester conurbation. It was so far out of the city that it was practically in Shropshire. It was so far that it was not even within my jurisdiction or even the jurisdiction of the Chester City police. It fell within the bounds of what they term 'Rural Cheshire,' a place *so* quiet it makes the city seem gangland.

Faulkner answered the door looking tired and bedraggled and exactly how you might expect someone to look had they recently got off a fourteen hour flight from Brazil. The only thing going against that fact was that she was so pale you wouldn't think she'd been anywhere at all.

"Hello." I said that in a strange, high pitched and unusual way, holding up my warrant card. "I'm D.I Simon Proctor. This is D.S Gershwin, We're here about…"

"The wild animal! Yes! Of course! Come in the pair of you." Faulkner pulled us both through the front door. "Is it too impertinent of me to ask you to take your shoes off?"

"Not at all Doctor Faulkner." We both kicked off our shoes.

"Please, call me Caroline. Sorry about the mess everywhere. I'm not usually this disorganised. Two weeks in Brazil and suddenly I'm all over the place."

"Did you hear about the rumour whilst you were out there?"

"Yes. My niece Zara told me about it over the phone the other day. She got it all from this internet star she's obsessed with."

"Jessie Hobb?" Gershwin and I asked together.

"Yes. How did you know? Would you like something to drink?"

"Tea, earl grey, hot," I said politely. "So long as there is one going."

"What about you D.S Gershwin?" Gershwin was examining some photographs on the wall.

"I'll have a coffee, thank you. These pictures, they're you with a jaguar aren't they?" Faulkner beamed.

"Yes. Thirty years ago. After I graduated I spent three years working at a sanctuary in Columbia. Best time of my life."

"You've kept up with the conservation work since?" We entered the kitchen, a country affair with old wood panelling, a range cooker and a big table which Gershwin and I sat down at.

"Mainly protecting jaguars who've ended up in this country. Idiots think they can keep them as pets but then they can't look after them and it all ends up very messy. Could be what you're looking at here."

"Not exactly. The picture that went viral… It isn't exactly… Well…" I took it out and placed it on the table where Faulkner could see it. She, rooting through a cupboard for some mugs, peered over her shoulder at it.

"Who would you like?" she asked whilst still trying to see the picture. "I've got William the Third, Queen Victoria... Maggie Thatcher for some reason... Oh, I know why! That was my ex-husband's..." I saw that the cupboard was full of mugs similar to those in Corwen's office. All big, three dimensional faces of famous people.

"Where did you get those?" I sprang, half excited that I might be able to replace the broken Gladstone.

"There's a shop in Stoke. I bought a whole box of them about five years ago. I'm sure the place is still there." If nothing else, I thought, this voyage out to the sticks had at least given me the prospect of a visit to this shop in Stoke and a replacement for the broken Gladstone.

"I'll have anybody except William the third," Gershwin grumbled, glaring at me as though I were Jessie Hobb.

"You got Gladstone? No? I'll have Cilla Black," I said, pointing to one on the end of the bottom shelf.

Mugs of tea and coffee brewed, Faulkner sat on the opposite side of the table and pulled the picture over to take a better look. She squinted, examined the smudge, and then shook her head.

"No. I'm sorry. That's definitely not a jaguar. If it's anything at all it's far too small for a jaguar."

"I'm glad you think so. Because we don't think *this* was a jaguar either." I took a sip of the tea. My mind was enchanted. This was the best tea, earl grey, hot, which I had ever tasted.

"So what's the trouble then?"

Gershwin and I both breathed deep before I revealed the answer to that question.

"There's been... An animal attack, I suppose you could call it. One... fatality." Doctor Faulkner was stricken.

"And you think *that* may be a jaguar?"

"It's possible..."

"Well if it was I can see how it might remain undetected. Rooftops! They're excellent climbers and one of them could prowl about up there, out of the way of people, and remain undetected."

Thank goodness the internet hadn't worked that one out. Our irritating Jeremy Beadle would have been scaling the walls and throwing things down at people, all the while shouting 'it's just a prank brah!' from on high.

"We don't think the jaguar *escaped* Doctor Faulkner,"

Gershwin told. Faulkner sat back and nodded.

"One of those pet owners then. It has to be. Some unthinking clot releasing it into the city because..." Gershwin held a hand up to silence her.

"There's no jaguar roaming the city centre at all... In fact, it's pretty clear that the body was dumped *after* being partially eaten."

"It *was* human?" Faulkner trembled. Gershwin and I both nodded and Faulkner got up to take a long walk around the kitchen. She looked desperately worried.

"We have reason to believe that somebody fed this person to the jaguar."

"Fed? As in, killed them and gave them over as meat? No that doesn't sound right. Jaguars are hunters, predators. They prefer to kill their own prey I mean, in captivity they *will* eat freshly butchered meat but mostly they prefer to stalk it."

"How fresh does the meat have to be?" I inquired.

"Shockingly fresh Mr Proctor. So fresh it has to have been butchered *within the hour* if at all possible."

"Not a week then?"

"A WEEK?" Doctor Faulkner sat down again and started

shaking her head.

"No... No... This cannot be a jaguar. I'm sorry. This has to be something else. Jaguars aren't carrion feeders. Do you by any chance have a picture I could see?"

"How strong is your stomach?"

"I've seen people killed in animal attacks, Mr Proctor. This should be no different." I pushed a picture of Gordon Gloucester's remains over. Faulkner took one brief look, was nearly sick, then pushed it back immediately. "No. That's not a jaguar. That's definitely not a jaguar. I don't know what this thing is... But it's not a jaguar."

"Are you absolutely sure?"

"Yes. If that was a jaguar the head would likely *not* still be attached. That... That could be anything... I don't know... It could be a predatory wildebeest for all I know!"

"If you know anybody who could be of help... A predatory wildebeest expert, if possible."

"There's a former colleague of mine, Professor Ingwe. He works at Cape Town University now." She checked her watch. "Cape Town is two hours ahead of us, I think... Would you like me to give him a ring?"

"If you could. It would be a great help to know what

we're dealing with," I pressed.

"Do you mind if I have a look around whilst I'm here," Gershwin diverted. I wondered what she was doing but Faulkner didn't raise an eyebrow. She nodded her consent and Gershwin wandered off.

It took a while for Faulkner to get an answer but eventually the phone was answered by a strong, friendly, African voice. Faulkner put the phone onto speaker.

"Ingwe... It's Caroline... Faulkner! How are you my old friend?"

"All the better for hearing your lovely voice again my dear. To what do I owe this pleasure?"

"I'm here with a police officer I'm afraid. He's having a bit of trouble identifying an animal attack. Looks like some bastard has been keeping something as a pet." She knew from a look I gave her not to say any more.

"Ahh... I see. What do you have to go on?"

"Well, for a start the head is still attached and this was definitely a carrion feeder."

"A carrion feeder? Your police officer friend must have something very nasty on his hands. Tell me, did the creature eat just muscle tissue or bone as well?"

"Both. And bits of suit," I intruded. "It ate everything it could." There was a deep, rattling breath on the other end of the line.

"We were thinking it might be a predatory wildebeest."

"No. Most certainly not. I've spent my life studying the behaviours of predatory wildebeest and I know for a fact that they are not carrion feeders." There was another deep, rattling breath, and then a long pause. "I may be wrong Caroline, but I think I *do* know what your police officer is looking for. And it is so very not good."

"What are we looking for?"

"A hyena, detective... A HYENA!"

EXHIBIT D: Hyena Hyena

I staggered out into the garden, feeling just as sick as I had done when I first looked at Gordon Gloucester's remains. Keeping a jaguar I might have just been able to understand. In a warped way they are cuddly, adorable, lovable. There is something graceful and beautiful about them. It is a deadly beauty, but quite often the most beautiful things are indeed deadly. I could justify to myself the idea that somebody might want to keep a jaguar for a pet, but a hyena? What twisted mind looks at a hyena and thinks they're beautiful or cool or in any way a nice animal? For a start they look like someone crossbred a dog with a pig. Then they open their mouths and start smiling in a way that makes them look like the craziest motherfuckers on the savannah. That's before I get to the wide eyed, evil glare. You can't read them, can't tell what they're thinking. Many animals have been claimed to have been sent by the devil, but hyenas are, in my opinion the most likely to be his minions.

"Are you alright Mr Proctor?" Faulkner had followed me

out and she was carrying a drink.

"Yes… I'll be over it in a second. A hyena? A God damned hyena? Somebody out there, in *my city* has a fucking hyena!" I didn't even want to say the rest of it. Feeding a corpse to a jaguar looked positively normal compared to this. This was sick. It was deluded.

"I've brought you a brandy if you want it," Faulkner offered.

"No… Thank you. I'm driving."

Gershwin came around the corner and saw us both. She looked nervous.

"What's going on?"

"Not a jaguar. A hyena!"

"A HYENA?" Gershwin nearly fell over. "We've got to sort this sir… Today… Before somebody else gets hurt."

"I agree," I said, trying to regain composure. I turned to Doctor Faulkner and smiled falsely, shaking her by the hand. "Doctor Faulkner, thank you for all your help. It's been a pleasure. I'll give you a call about that shop in Stoke."

I hastened to the car and had my seatbelt on and the engine ready before Gershwin had got to the door. Now was not the time for Whitney so I cut the CD player as soon as it started up.

"Is the next stop St Blaise's, sir?"

"Yes. This... I don't even know what this is any more. Whatever it is it has become sick and twisted and somehow Jeremy Beadle is wrapped up in it all, as is St Blaise's church."

"That Doctor Faulkner as well," Gershwin suggested. I gave her a puzzled glance. "Did she look like she'd been in Brazil to you?"

"Maybe she doesn't tan. Perhaps she's been so busy inside the conference centre that she hasn't had a chance to sunbathe. Did you find anything?"

"Not a thing, though there are outbuildings that would be the perfect place to keep something like a hyena. Don't you find it suspicious that she had the number for someone who *knew* what we were looking at?"

"She's a wild animal expert. She has contacts. Unless you're suggesting that her friend Professor Ingwe is involved as well?"

"Could be. How do we know he's really in Cape Town?"

"We don't... I suppose..."

"Precisely. And she knew about Hobb. She *knew* about Hobb!"

"Her niece, as she said," I protested. "And where's the connection to Gordon Gloucester? To St Blaise's church?"

"She could be a parishioner." She could… But trying to tie Doctor Faulkner into this was never going to work. "You fancied her as well."

"And that makes her guilty?"

"Not denying it then?"

"No. How did you know?"

"You had a misty look in your eyes the whole time you were there, from the moment she opened the door. And as for when she opened that mug cupboard… You could go off to that shop in Stoke as a first date!" Gershwin was mocking so I tried to ignore her. "Well… You could take her there but it would have to be before you arrested her for feeding Gloucester to a hyena."

"We don't know it was her!" Gershwin folded her arms and stared out the window in silence. Something had put a bee up her skirt. She had latched onto Faulkner as a suspect and, ignoring all evidence, had decided she was the one. It was a bad way to do policing. You've got to keep an open mind. Everyone is innocent until the evidence categorically confirms them as guilty.

Less than ten minutes later we pulled up outside St Blaise's church. One of those red, Cheshire sandstone monoliths. Not a beautiful looking church but old with a cemetery that was packed with tumble down tombstones and long grass. The main thing I didn't like about it was that the builders hadn't been able to decide if they wanted a tower or a spire and had tried to combine the two. They failed and the church had ended up looking as if a Soviet observation post had been tacked onto one end.

Greensborough Dewdrop was walking the path to the door and turned around when he heard my car pull up to the pavement. He lifted himself up onto his tiptoes to see who it was and he recognised me. I saw his face twist into a downward sneer and then he came striding towards us, a nasty pounce to his step.

"Simon Proctor. To what do I owe this intrusion?" I stood up as tall as I could, towering over that horrible little man.

"Let's see. How about we start with the fact that your church is at the centre of a nasty business involving a wild animal, one of your recently deceased parishioners, and a

Jeremy Beadle wannabe who goes to the nom-de-plume of Ubi-Hobb-Throb. I'm hoping you can tell me what is going on."

"Ubi-Hobb-Throb? Is he that disgusting little wretch who was prowling around my churchyard the other day?"

"You know damn well he is," I replied. "You know damn well because, just maybe, one of your young female parishioners has told you about him. Or maybe you spend your evenings keeping up *wid da kidz* and watching popular internet videos. Or, just maybe, his disgusted cameraman told you?"

That last one caused a twitch above Dewdrop's left eyebrow, exactly the sign I was looking for.

"I didn't speak to that other person." Dewdrop spat as he spoke. "All I know is what Hobb shouted at him after he dropped the camera."

"And what did he shout?"

"He said he was going to get him, said he was going to bring him down. Called him Icepicks."

"What day was this?" Gershwin jumped in. "The day Hobb turned up and started throwing dung, I mean."

"It was two days ago. We'd just buried someone very dear

to us. To myself and Timmy."

"And that's why you both looked upset on the video?"

"You've seen it?" Dewdrop looked frightened.

"Yes. Hobb uploaded it last night, in complete breach of his bail conditions." Dewdrop mumbled something about Hobb being a little shit. Unpriestly behaviour. "The person you buried... It was Gordon Gloucester?" Dewdrops's eyes bulged.

"Gloucester was a dear friend. His death was an absolute... An absolute piece of... A travesty! I told him to buy a new boiler but he kept saying he'd keep it till it broke. Well it did break and it killed him."

"Mr Dewdrop, may we go inside the church? We have some hard news for you."

"No. You may not come into my church. If you have anything to say you can say it out here."

"Very well. The reason Hobb came to our attention was that he was attempting to sniff around a crime scene for video views."

"Typical! I hope you throw the book at the little... person."

"You seem particularly animus towards Hobb," Gershwin

said.

"He threw dung at me. Of course I'm animus towards him... And he threw dung at Timmy. He was shell shocked. It was made worse by the fact that we had just buried Gordon."

"Did many people come to the funeral? Any other parishoners?"

"It was myself, Timmy and a few of our WI ladies. That was all."

"And you are absolutely sure that you buried him two days ago? That he was in the coffin that went into the ground?"

"Yes. Of course. Why wouldn't he be?"

"This crime scene Hobb was sniffing around... *Somebody* had dumped Gordon Gloucester's chewed up remains in the middle of the city centre."

"Impossible," Dewdrop scoffed. "He *was* in that coffin. He was in our crypt overnight. He wanted to spend his last night here before going up to heaven."

"And you couldn't resist a peek?"

"It was an open casket."

"I see. May we look at this crypt? Just round the back

isn't it?"

Before Dewdrop could protest I had wandered off across the churchyard, through the tumbledown graves, looking for any sign of a recent burial along the way. There was one, unmarked, in the far corner, where there was a clean cut oblong of finely raked and pressed down soil. The last resting place of, something, but not Gordon Gloucester. In the nearby distance I could hear drilling, building work, the sound of rubble being thrown into a skip.

Interesting.

"What time was the funeral, if you don't mind me asking?" Gershwin interrogated. She and Dewdrop were following me across the churchyard.

"Half ten in the morning. Not that it is of any consequence."

"And the Hobb incident was shortly afterwards? Before mid-day?"

"Yes. I believe so."

"You believe so?" Gershwin stopped, stunned. "You only *believe* so? You can't remember when somebody threw a steaming turd at you?"

"It *was* before midday, yes."

"You don't sound too certain of that, Mr Dewdrop." Dewdrop did not say anything, as was unfortunately his right.

I had reached the entrance to the crypt. All there was in the way of a door was a metal grating and beyond that some tricksy looking steps which someone might easily slip down. There looked to be no latch or lock on the grating.

"Couldn't anyone have got down here in the night? How do you keep this door secure?"

"There is a padlock," Dewdrop sniffed snobbishly.

"If there's a padlock then where is it?" I searched the grass that was growing around the corners of the crypt entrance to see if it had fallen off. There was no sign of it. "Mr Dewdrop… When did you last see Gloucester's body? Answer *very* carefully… Because *somehow* Gloucester's body ended up in the centre of Chester less than twenty four hours after he was reportedly buried. Now either somebody came here, in the dead of night, with a spade, and dug him up, or they took his body from this crypt and you buried something else."

"What else would I bury, Mr Proctor?" I pointed in the direction of the drilling noise.

"That? Building rubble! Wouldn't be too difficult for someone to go skip diving to replace the body with an equal weight."

I swung open the grate and started downwards into the crypt. These steps were awkward, old and treacherous. It was hard to imagine any funeral directors would be willing to allow their staff to carry a coffin down here. I also reckoned that they might have a few things to say about the matter of security.

Nor was it a nice crypt. It was dark, dingy, and there was a torrid smell. The only light was dim, filtered through some old and cracked stained glass high up on one wall. There was no way anybody who knew this place would want to spend their last night down here, dead or alive. Anyone who wanted to spend their last night in the church would prefer to be above, in the main building.

"Gloucester was kept down here overnight, was he?" Dewdrop uttered not a sound. Gershwin took a wander around, examining the place, and then stepped in something.

"I'm not buying it," she admitted, trying to see what was on her shoe. "No funeral director would bring a coffin down here. It's too damp, too smelly…" I heard a derisive snort from Dewdrop.

Returning back to the light of the churchyard, I watched as Gershwin started wiping her shoe against the long grass that was by the entrance to the crypt. She began muttering something about dog shit. There was more of it in the grass near one of the graves, I noticed.

"Why *is* your churchyard so full of poo, Mr Dewdrop?"

"Some disgusting local I shouldn't wonder… Walking their dog around the church and not cleaning up after it."

"They've got into the crypt as well as by the look of it," Gershwin cursed. "Seriously… You need a lock on that place." Seeing that her wiping was doing little good she removed the shoe. It was covered in a lot of poo.

"Whoever owns that dog, it must have a serious diarrhoea problem!"

"Have you quite finished here?" Dewdrop demanded.

"No. We haven't. There's the matter of how Gordon Gloucester's body ended up in the city centre to figure out. We'd also like to speak to your son about the incident with Jessie Hobb."

"No. I refuse," Dewdrop defied.

"You have no choice, Mr Dewdrop." That was not strictly true, though I didn't want to tell him that. Seeing as he had no good reason to refuse and was just being obstructive, I thought it for the best if I overruled him.

"You cannot interview a minor without a consenting adult present,' Dewdrop complained.

"No, Mr Dewdrop. Just an adult. Doesn't have to be consenting." You didn't even need that, if I was being absolutely honest, though it does usually help.

"I'll have your badge for this you low born scoundrel," Dewdrop threatened.

"Fantastic! Early retirement will suit me fine," I deflected. "Now… Is Timothy in the church?" A petulant look from Dewdrop signalled that he was.

I headed straight for the church, defying Dewdrop's protests.

This may not have been entirely appropriate behaviour, overriding the wishes of a member of the clergy and what not, but I wasn't going to back down in the face of this awful man. I wanted to see him suffer, to see him flounce about and whinge and cry that I was abusing my authority. It gave me a kick, a thrill, and I didn't much care if he made an official complaint. The expression on Gershwin's face, she was now holding her dirty shoe and hobbling behind, said that she would back me to the hilt. Dewdrop was an obsequious bully with a superiority complex. The further he was brought down the better.

Timothy, or Timmy as Dewdrop the Elder insisted upon calling him, was absolutely the opposite. If I hadn't known, and if they hadn't both had the same kind of fat, squashed nose and pointy chin, I'd have bet money that the late Madame Dewdrop had once had a fling with the man who comes to read the gas meter.

Timothy was sat on the floor of the church, sorting through a bag of papers and arranging them in piles.

"Timmy," Dewdrop the Elder puffed. "This gentleman is from the police. He'd like to talk to you about what happened the other day with that… that person throwing the poo!" Timothy smiled up at me. I sat down on the floor beside him, not a wise thing to do at my age for there was every chance I might not be able to get back up again. I looked at the papers he was sorting. They all appeared to be drawings, some of them good and some of them awful.

"These are all from Mr Gloucester's animal club,"

Timothy explained. "I'm finding the best so I can make a display." He didn't take his eyes off the pictures or stop sorting through them.

"I like this one," I pointed to a one of a hedgehog snuffling through some leaves. Timothy smiled and moved it onto another of the piles.

"Yes. I like that one too." He showed me one that he had put to the side of him. "This was mine." The picture was a 'Noah's Ark' tableaux, with kangaroos and tigers and Zebras and an awful lot of dogs.

"Do you like dogs?"

"Oh yes. I love dogs. I love all animals."

"Did Mr Gloucester like animals too?" Timothy nodded.

"Mr Gloucester loved animals. He bred hedgehogs and dogs.' Dewdrop coughed from where he had arranged himself on the nearest pew.

"If you could keep this brief, Mr Proctor."

"Timothy... When your father discovered Mr Gloucester's body... Were you there as well?"

"Yes. It wasn't very nice." I decided not to dwell on that subject.

"And the boy who threw poo at you the other day? Do

you know who he was?"

"Yes. Isherwood told me."

"Isherwood?"

"Isherwood... He was very kind. He helped us after the boy threw the poo. He made sure we were alright."

"Was Isherwood the cameraman?" Timothy gave a slow nod.

"Do you know what his last name was?"

"Spicks," Timothy said clearly.

Isherwood Spicks... Of course... I. Spicks... Icepicks! With a name that unusual he wouldn't be hard to find.

"One more question Timothy, if you don't mind. The night before you buried him, where was Gordon Gloucester's coffin?" I saw there was a terror in his eyes, as though a great beast had just caught hold of him.

"He was in the crypt," he told me, uncertainly, unconfidently. I let it drop. Instead of pressing the matter further I picked my creaking bones up from the floor and made for the exit of the church, Dewdrop the Elder and Gershwin hobbling behind.

"I trust this will be the last I'll be seeing of you, Mr Proctor?" Dewdrop grumbled as I reached the car.

"Not on your nelly Mr Dewdrop. I'll be back with an exhumation order as soon as I get one. I want to make sure Gordon Gloucester isn't in his grave." There was a worried and angry expression upon Dewdrop's face.

Back in the car Gershwin held up her poo covered shoe.

"Do you have a bag I can put this in?" I pointed to the glove box where I kept a stash of spare evidence bags.

"I don't believe him about the local with the diarrhoea dog," I said as we drove off.

"You think it was the hyena? A hyena with diarrhoea?"

"Think about this... Gordon Gloucester... His body was taken from the church, according to Dewdrop. So... Either somebody took his body away to be eaten by the hyena, or the hyena was *there at the church.*"

"Interesting theory sir. But why did the hyena have diarrhoea?"

"That I do not know... But there is one definite way to find out if my theory is correct. If we get Pearson to analyse the poo on your shoe he might be able to find out if it came from a hyena or a dog."

"He's going to *love* that!" Gershwin drawled.

"After having to stare at Gloucester's body a bit of hyena

poo is going to be like living in paradise."

Gloucester's home address was our final call. Tarvin was quiet, dead, nobody around, exactly as a suburban village should be at that time in the morning. The only people walking around were old ladies with tartan shopping trolleys. They paid us no heed, just went about their day as though it were normal to see a third rate sports car driving past them.

As Gershwin and I pulled up to the pavement the first thing we saw was Gloucester's car. A twenty year old *Hyundai Excel*. It was parked badly, half across the lawn and half on the drive, as though whoever had put it there had been in a rush. From what little I knew Gloucester didn't seem the type to park in such a haphazard way, especially not over his own drive. He seemed like the sort of man who, even if he were flustered or hurrying, would make sure he parked dead straight and proper.

I confirmed this by peering through the window of the front room. Everything was neat and ordered, very tidy. The carpets were clean, there was no litter or magazines or anything lying around. There was a place for everything and everything was in its place.

I headed back to the car, got down on my knees and looked underneath. The ground was wet, very wet, not bone dry as it ought to have been.

Gershwin, meanwhile, had decided to go diving through Gloucester's bins. Last week had been a recycling collection so the waste was almost full. From the bin she pulled a small white bag enclosing another small white bag within which was yet more, by now very smelly and very mouldy, poo. Gershwin did not look happy about holding it.

"Detective Sergeant Gershwin," I said, getting up off the ground and wiping myself down, "we are going to need a search warrant."

Two hours, a trip up to Blacon to deposit Gershwin's poo shoe and the bag found in the bin, and we were back at Gloucester's house with Pearson, the warrant and a few uniforms to keep what few people there were at bay. We gained entry by way of a neighbour who had a spare key.

It is never nice, entering the empty house of somebody who has recently died. All their possessions are still there, exactly where they last left them. The ghost of the person is hanging around. It is not like they've died at all. It's like they've gone on holiday. At such times I always feel like an intruder, like I'm not supposed to be there. Most police work I enjoy, even if some of it is in a perverted way, but entering the homes of the deceased is never enjoyable.

"What are we looking for?" Pearson asked, shining a UV torch around. There were smudged fingerprints on everything.

"Signs of a hyena and of somebody who isn't Gloucester."

"Somebody who isn't Gloucester might be difficult. This place will have been trudged through by police and paramedics when they found the body."

"True. But I suspect there will be something more recent than that."

We headed up the stairs, looking through a notepad by the telephone along the way. There was a phone number, the name Bathsheeba Badoing, and underneath an underlined

'*Cheshire Wildlife Trust,*' on the first page. Most of the rest of the upstairs was nothing. A bedroom, a room full of junk, the bathroom. There was the study, however, and Pearson immediately moved to examine the keyboard.

"If this is where the tweet to Hobb was sent from, the prints of whoever sent this…" He snapped on a pair of gloves and began extracting the top layer of prints.

"Mightn't whoever sent the tweet have sent it from their own mobile?"

"Possible, D.S Gershwin, possible. But they'd have first had to access Gloucester's account, even if it was just to get the password."

Whilst he was getting on with the job I checked all the upstairs windows for sign of forced entry. They were all locked from the inside and all opened only a tiny smish, barely enough to squeeze a hand through.

Finding no sign of entry, I went to check downstairs, being careful not to touch anything, and found not a sign there either. Whoever had been in here had a key of some kind.

By the kitchen sink I noticed a glass, empty apart from the dregs of some brown liquid. I left it for Pearson to take a look at and instead took a gander in the fridge. On the top shelf was an unappetising, cling filmed bowl of raw meat. It resembled beef. More interesting was the milk in the shelf on the door. This was fresh, so fresh that it might have been bought two days ago. It was three days ago actually, as I discovered by opening the pedal bin next to the back door. There was a receipt lying on the top of a lot of rotting vegetable peelings. Gordon Gloucester certainly didn't buy that milk, though it was local, bought from a shop on Tarvin High Street. Whoever had bought it also smoked as they'd gotten a packet of cigarettes as well.

Though a small thing, this was more useful than all the fingerprints and DNA evidence in the world. That shop would have CCTV and with a time stamped receipt I could finger and identify exactly who had bought this milk and those cigarettes.

I showed the receipt to Pearson who was coming down the stairs. He sniffed it.

"Has this been in the bin? Christ, I don't envy your job one bit Simon. I may have to prod through mouldering corpses but at least I don't have to go rooting through bins! Did you find anything else?"

"Glass of something by the sink. The milk from *that* receipt... Not much else."

"Have you tried the garage?"

Pearson went for a door between the kitchen and the hall. It was locked, but it didn't take long to find the key in a draw. The light switched on, both of us sighed. There wasn't much in here apart from three cat carrying cages, all open, and a couple of dog bowls that were filled with stagnant waters. Pearson discovered some strands of fur that had got caught in one of the cage doors and started bagging it up.

"DNA testing should tell us if this matches the poo."

"Bit small for a hyena these," I pointed out. I was starting to look through a chest freezer in the corner of the room. There seemed to be an awful lot of beef in there, a staggering amount.

"Could have had them for when the hyena was a puppy... Or whatever you call young hyenas."

"Then why are there three of them?"

"Sir." Gershwin was in the door waving a portable sat nav. "Found this in the glove box of the car."

"The last journey?"

"The last journey!" She started playing with the buttons and came up with a history. Two days ago that sat-nav had been programmed with a journey from our present location to the back of Crook Street. The strange thing was the time. Half seven in the evening. Before Gloucester's body had been dumped.

I passed the sat-nav to Pearson.

"That can't be right. Either you're looking at a dead end or somebody trying to clever."

"My money is on somebody trying to be clever. Have you checked the boot yet?"

"Allow me," Pearson offered, leaving by way of the garage door.

Gershwin tossed him the keys and Pearson, hands in pockets, strode to the back of the car. He paused for a second after unlocking the boot and left it hanging a millimetre from springing up.

"This is going to be bad," he warned.

It was.

That boot was covered with small, half chewed up bits of Gordon Gloucester.

EXHIBIT E: Suus Iustus A Ludo, Brah

Everything fell into place. At least everything that involved the dumping of the body. The receipt led to a CCTV image of the person who had bought the milk. A picture shown to Gloucester's neighbours revealed that person had been there two days before and that the car had been missing for an entire night and most of the day before. The same person was seen returning it early in the evening, parking it haphazardly, and hurrying away.

We returned to the CCTV of Crook Street. The car appeared at quarter to eight the evening before the discovery. But then our suspect, who was clearly visible in the driving seat, just walked away, away down Watergate Street. From what we could tell the body hadn't been dumped. If it had, according to Pearson, the person would have been covered in bits of Gloucester, just like the boot of the car was.

I immediately knew what had happened, and it was as I said. The person had tried to be clever. They had tried to move in such a way so as to avoid detection, but as always in such cases they had failed to outsmart the police.

There was no sign of the body dumping on CCTV, no sign of anybody entering Crook Street at the appropriate time, but an idea of Gershwin's saw us discover the full solution to that one. We required yet more CCTV footage, this time of the crossing at Northgate Street, but we soon had them. As Pearson predicted they looked to be a bit blood soaked. They had only managed to get away with that, I thought, because it was the middle of the night.

From Gloucester's neighbours we had a rough idea of when the car was returned, which happened to be long *after* the body had been discovered. The cheeky little bastard had actually left Gloucester's car *at* Crook Street and collected it later. It had been there the whole time, and we missed it. This fact was confirmed by the footage Hobb had filmed whilst sneaking around the crime scene. Gloucester's car was right there in the background, number plate perfectly visible, parked right next to the entrance to the alleyway.

There were still questions to be answered, lots of questions. Why? Why dump the body there and lure Hobb to the scene? What did Hobb have to do with any of this? How had the body been taken, and when? Where did our hyena fit into it? The answers, I hoped, as well as with the numerous phone calls and enquiries that were going on around me, would lie with Isherwood Spicks.

He came into the station voluntarily. Hobb, the little git, had his father tweet that he'd been arrested (he was actually referring to a re-arrest following the breech in his bail conditions) and to say that he wouldn't be allowed to upload any more videos due to 'corrupt and tyrannical policeman.' It really did say *policeman* and not policemen. I took that as a personal affront, believing that it was directly referring to myself. Seeing this, Spicks decided he wanted to confess his involvement with Hobb's rampage of inanity.

When I first clapped eyes on him, in the reception area filling out a form, I could see in his eyes that the guilt was eating him away. Must have been eating away at him for some time. He was older than Hobb, by at least three years, and was more clean cut, much more sensible, average all over. It made his part in all this lunacy that much more difficult to accept.

"Why would somebody like you want to hang out with a would be Jeremy Beadle like Hobb?"

"Jeremy Beadle?" Spicks looked at me confused. I

wondered how on earth he could not know who Jeremy Beadle was.

"He was a television prankster," I said. "Much like Hobb and all these other internet morons. Only there was *one* difference. Beadle had a conscience! He didn't go around screaming at strangers or throwing muck at people. Alright, some of his pranks might have been a bit cruel, especially at the end of his career, but at least he stuck around to face the consequences. He didn't run away screaming 'it's just a prank brah,' at the top of his voice." Spicks sniffed a guilty sniff. "So… Going to answer my question? Why would someone like *you* want to hang around with Hobb? You don't look the kind of person who'd hurt someone for fun."

"I'm not. I don't *like* hurting people."

"That's what you did though. You're an accomplice in Hobb's assault spree. You looked on as he made people miserable. You filmed it. Then he went and put the footage on the internet, as if reducing people to tears wasn't enough. How many people do you think laughed at those videos? Laughed at other people's misery? How many subscribers does he have? Twelve million! TWELVE MILLION PEOPLE LAUGHING AT *INNOCENT*

PEOPLE BEING REDUCED TO TEARS!"

"It was fun, at first," Spicks admitted.

"Fun?"

"At first... When he wasn't so cruel. He didn't hurt people to start with. He just acted like a bit of an idiot. The joke was on him, not other people."

"For example?"

"He walked round a shopping centre crying and telling people he'd lost his mummy. He tried to perform a concert in the middle of a duck pond."

"And people *liked* that? It sounds vacuous!" Spicks twiddled his thumbs and shuffled nervously.

"People did like it... And Hobb got more and more... His ideas got more and more wild and he started doing really cruel things like screaming at people and throwing things at them."

"You weren't such a fan of this?"

"No."

"But you still went with it?"

"Hobb is earning bucket loads and he's been throwing stuff my way. I've been getting a cut. Five hundred pounds for a couple of hours filming sometimes."

"Can anybody get in on this game? Five hundred pounds for a couple of hours work would make a nice addendum to my pension!"

"You *could*..." Spicks seemed unsure about that. Maybe he didn't like the idea of a cop making internet videos, or someone of my age making internet videos. I had no intention of starting, however. It wasn't my thing.

"The money was more important to you than other people's well-being? Their happiness?"

"I thought it was. But these last couple of months Hobb has got really, really bad. He thinks he's untouchable. He thinks he's some kind of prankster god."

"Jeremy Beadle is the prankster god. Don't you *dare* even put Hobb in the same league as him," I warned.

"I filmed a video for him a few weeks ago. He'd rented a couple of quad bikes. I thought we might have a nice ride, do something a bit stupid. Then Hobb decided he wanted to use them to absolutely *wreck* a farmer's field. I wouldn't do it. I wouldn't film him doing that. I dropped the camera and walked away."

"Where was this? Did he actually *wreck* the field in the end?"

"I don't think he did, no. But that night he called me up. Said if I didn't film his pranks for him he'd get me."

"Get you? Get you how?" Spicks reached into his pocket and pulled out a flash drive.

"I didn't know he'd filmed it… Honest… I went round to his house whilst he was out and pretended I'd left something behind. I was going to destroy it but…"

"Do I want to know *what the fuck* is on this flash drive?" I gave Spicks a withering glare. Spicks didn't answer me.

"Is it bad?"

"It's bad," Spicks gulped.

"Is it the only copy?"

"As far as I'm aware. After the poo thing Hobb found out it was gone and he rang me up and started ranting about how he was going to fit me up for stealing it. He threatened to break into my house and plant kiddy porn onto my computer." I knew that trick from Corwen's lot. They called it the *Edmonds Protocol*.

"Let me give you something," I told him. "I've never heard you mention this flash drive. As far as I am aware it doesn't exist. I don't know what is on it and believe me I don't want to know. You're in enough trouble as it is without adding this to the mix as well. Right?" Spicks nodded and removed the offending flash drive from sight. "Now tell me about the day Hobb threw the poo at Dewdrop and his son."

"I'd had enough. It was disgusting. He'd flipped. Throwing poo at someone… I couldn't stand it anymore. I'd had enough of him. I wasn't going to play his silly little games anymore."

"What happened after you dropped the camera? What did you do?"

"Hobb tried to fight me. I floored him. Knocked his knees out from under him and then threw the camera back at him. I told him to clear off and he said he was going to get me."

"Timothy Dewdrop says you helped him and his father. Is that correct?"

"Yes. I made sure they were ok, helped them clean the poo from the door of the church and from around the churchyard. I think there was a funeral that afternoon. Somebody they were close to…"

"Sorry… Did you say *afternoon*?" Spicks nodded. I urged him to carry on. "How did they seem to you? The Dewdrops?

"That reverend... Tim's father... I noticed he was a bit... He seemed really upset. For a while he just sat on a pew covered in poo."

"Like he was in shock, you mean?"

"Yes. He went away to clean himself up but he seemed to be gone an awfully long time. Then he asked me all sorts of questions about Hobb and what he was doing."

"You told him? You told him about the internet videos and the jaguar obsession? You told him *who* Hobb is?" Spicks gave an affirmative bow.

"For a priest he didn't seem very understanding. He said some very nasty things to me about my filming it all."

"Maybe he was right. You're old enough to know better. I know it wasn't you who threw the poo or assaulted those people, but you're still complicit."

I was trying to be understanding but every so often a surge of anger was coming into my voice. Spicks *should* have known better. He should have reined Hobb in a long time ago, walked away a long time ago. He should not have stood by and let it all happen. For that there would be consequences.

For all our actions, be they good or bad, there should be

consequences. When we are involved in something foul, as Spicks was involved in this foul thing, no matter by how much, we must take responsibility for our portion of the blame and we must hold our hands up and face the music. Fair play to Spicks, he did admit he was in the wrong and he was willingly facing the music, but how long had it taken him to do so? Too long in my opinion.

Even Hobb's regular viewers, his so called fans, held some of the blame. They continued to watch him, to support him as he did those awful things. Though, reading through the video comments, there were some who rightly made their protestations known they were always shot down with a torrent of abuse from Hobb's die-hard groupies. The words 'it's just a prank brah,' came up with disturbing regularity. The fans refused to see that the thing they were watching was cruel, was senseless, was immoral. They went with it, fuelled Hobb as he grew out of control. What consequences there would be for those die-hards I didn't know, I didn't know what consequences there *could* be.

I hope there were some, somewhere.

I left the interview room for a break, left Spicks to think about what else he wanted to say. There didn't seem to be much I could get out of him, only what I already knew. I must have been deep in thought. I didn't even notice that my phone had rung. Only when I checked my missed call register half an hour later did I notice that it was Corwen.

I was still thinking when Gershwin whapped me on the nut with a tablet. It hurt. I looked at her, disgruntled.

"Team have done with the exhumation at St Blaise's," she said.

"And? Anything good?"

"Oh yes! Three baby hyenas. All of them dead and lying on top of a thin layer of building rubble and a bit more of Gordon Gloucester."

"Dead?" I said, baffled. "Why would the hyenas be..." I realised before I finished speaking.

I started to laugh. Of course they were dead! It made perfect sense that they were dead.

It didn't take a genius to work out why. Now I knew everything and the whole parade of lunacy made perfect sense. I saw everything, every strand, from the viral photograph of the jaguar through to why Hobb was lured to the crime scene.

"D.S Gershwin," I said boldly. "I want Hobb, Parsons,

Spicks and both Dewdrops outside the jaguar enclosure of Chester Zoo!"

"Not Caroline Faulkner, sir?"

"No. I was right about her. Too much time in the conference centre to get a tan!" Gershwin started to walk away but turned back.

"If I may be so bold. Why do you want them all outside the jaguar enclosure?"

"Because I'm in just the right mood for showing off," I told her.

Jessie Hobb. Andrew Parsons. Isherwood Spicks. Timothy Dewdrop. Greensborough Dewdrop. All five of them sat in a semi-circle, glaring at me as I paced up and down in front of the jaguar enclosure.

"Gentlemen," I began. "To begin at the beginning, with the jaguar. He is the only innocent in all this nonsense. The only reason he *is* innocent is because he does not exist. He never existed. He was a smudge in the background of a photograph taken outside St Blaise's church. Yet if it were not for that imaginary jaguar, if not for that photograph and for the idiots on the internet proclaiming there was a big cat on the loose, then the crimes I am here to reveal would remain unknown or not have passed at all. You, Isherwood Spicks, may never have left the side of Jessie Hobb. You might still be his loyal cameraman, wondering whether or not to walk away, but still filming his antics. You, Jessie Hobb, the would be Jeremy Beadle…"

"Who's Jeremy Beadle?" Hobb looked at everyone else, confused.

"You, Jessie Hobb, the would be Jeremy Beadle, would still be stood on high, continuing your reign of terror until someone grew the balls to bring you down. You would not, if it weren't for the jaguar, have gone to St Blaise's and you would not have flung muck at the Dewdrops. And Gordon Gloucester? He'd be in his grave right now. Nobody would have ever known that one of you five had fed his remains to three baby hyenas."

I watched them all.

"There was not one crime here. It would take a perverted mind to conceive of all this as one crime. No. What we are looking at are a series of crimes, each as a consequence of another. In this chain of crime you all played your part. You are *all* guilty."

"Guilty?" Parsons spluttered. "What have I done? I've done nothing!"

"But you *have,* Mr Parsons. You may not have committed a crime in any legal sense but when it comes to crime of the moral sense, the social sense, you're as guilty as everybody else here. I refer, of course, to your son and your responsibility for your son. As his father it was your duty to see him brought up good and proper, to make sure he behaved like a responsible citizen.

"There are, I think, two strands to crime. There are those crimes that hurt people, that cause injury and grief. Crimes like stealing, murder, speeding down the motorway drunk, at three in the morning... But then there are crimes that disrupt the order and running of civilisation, crimes that are against the nature of humanity. Crimes like fraud. Like improper disposal of a body. Letting your dog foul on the pavement, or in some cases in the middle of a churchyard and not cleaning it up. Most crimes are against the law, especially in the first instance. Some of the latter ones aren't. They are only crimes against morality, and what you have committed, Mr Parsons, is a crime against morality.

"YOU allowed your son free reign to cause anarchy. YOU didn't reel him in from his spree of blatant abuses and assaults and lord only knows whatever else. YOU let it happen. YOU excused his behaviour. Your job was to *stop him* from doing stupid stuff like that, if not for his sake then for the sake of society. You failed, Mr Parsons. You failed so hard they'll still be feeling your failure at the end of the next millennium."

"And I suppose you brought *your* son up all good and proper didn't you?" Dewdrop the Elder sneered. "You couldn't even give him a proper name!"

"Corwen is a better name than Greensborough, Mr Dewdrop… Besides which, his name was his mother's choice."

"Is he still a bandit? Still a rogue and a wastrel? How many children does he have now? By how many women? Three? Four? I bet he doesn't care for any of them…"

"No children at present, Mr Dewdrop," I smiled. "But I spoke to him not ten minutes ago and he *is* going to care about his child because he's decided to stick it through. We can expect Felinheli Naismith-Proctor to arrive in about seven months."

"Felinheli?"

"A pin in a map, Mr Hobb… A pin in a map! But back to the matter at hand. The crimes! And *your* crimes, Mr Hobb, we all know of. You're famous. A young internet superstar. You got there through ungodly means. You got there through being the most evil little squit to disgrace the Welsh borders since Jack Falstaff…"

"Is he like Jeremy Beadle?"

"Go brush up on your Shakespeare, Mr Hobb. Jack Falstaff was a rogue, a villain and a coward. Besides a pot belly and tendency towards alcoholism the two of you are similar. It takes a special brand of cowardice to assault people… No… Not just to assault people… To assault people *for fun*! You did it for shits and giggles. You got a kick out of it.

"Reports were made by the way. A lady in Connah's Quay whom you shot with a water pistol. She has a fear of open spaces, agoraphobia. She was starting to get better and then you jumped out on her and set her back months, maybe years. You, Hobb, *hurt* people. You *assaulted* people, innocent people, and then ran away screaming 'It's just a prank brah!' That is not an excuse for anything. There is even less of an excuse to film that assault and put it on the internet... Which is where you come in, Mr Spicks."

"Jessie Hobb's loyal cameraman, there by his side as his rampage progressed, complicit in everything he did. Oh, you started to feel guilty, but far too late to do any good. You only did the right thing after it was too late. You only broke ranks when he did something so abhorrent it could only take a sick mind to stand by him after that...

"But I'm getting ahead of myself. What were the two of you doing in St Blaise's churchyard in the first place? The answer is obvious. The jaguar! The innocent imaginary jaguar without whom we would know nothing, and none of this would have happened. You, Hobb, had become *obsessed* with that jaguar. You couldn't get enough. Anything to do with that jaguar, you were there. So of course, you had to go to where the photo was taken. You had to see for yourself.

"But that, Mr Hobb, was your undoing. You did something so despicable that not only did your previously loyal cameraman finally turn on you, but your assault spree unintentionally collided head on with another crime and created yet another crime in itself, which bring us all here today.

"The churchyard was covered in poo, lots of it, and you were in your element, Mr Hobb. You smeared the church door with it, threw it at the two Dewdrops. You thought it was jaguar poo, but you couldn't have been more wrong. That was no jaguar poo. It was *hyena* poo!

"How in the name of anything that is holy does hyena poo end up all over a British churchyard *and* inside the crypt? The answer, lies with Gordon Gloucester.

"There was a number, beside his phone, for Bathsheeba Badoing of the Cheshire Wildlife Trust. All it took was a phone call to find the reason why.

"Gordon Gloucester, animal lover, was, of course, a volunteer for the aforementioned Cheshire Wildlife Trust. Mrs Badoing helpfuly informed us that a few weeks ago an old lady by the name of Gladys Godfrey was walking in Delamere Forest when she found a hessian bag, dumped in the undergrowth by the side of the path. It was wriggling so she opened it up. What did she find? Three baby hyenas! Some twisted fool, lord knows who, had illegally imported these creatures, or maybe their mother. Perhaps to sell on as exotic pets. Then they callously left them in the forest to die. Mrs Godfrey reported the find, of course she did, and the wildlife trust collected the hyenas. BUT they did not have the resources to look after them. They deal with badgers and ferrets and drop squirrels. They aren't capable of looking after hyenas. So until they could find someone to take the hyenas off their hands, they passed them to one of their volunteers, Gordon Gloucester.

"Gloucester gave them the run of his garage, bought them cat cages to transport them to wherever they would be taken next, fed them on beef, which we found in his freezer.

"Then Gordon Gloucester died. His ancient boiler was pumping out Carbon Monoxide and he fell into a deep sleep and died. No dependencies. Not many friends. Only a few people in the whole world who would miss him. Only *two* who really would- The Dewdrops.

"You were the one Gloucester charged with wrapping up his estate, were you not, Mr Dewdrop?"

Dewdrop the Elder made no movement. "There's no point denying it because I checked with the coroner's office. It was up to you to carry out Gloucester's final wishes, to see that his affairs were set in order. You didn't do a good job, in all fairness, as it seems you neglected to inform the Cheshire Wildlife Trust that he had passed away.

"They found someone to take the hyenas, a specialist who works at Knowsley. When they tried to contact Gloucester they couldn't reach him. Nobody was answering the phone and when they went round to his house there was nobody there. There wasn't even a sign of the hyenas... Or not that they could find anyway. They had begun making enquiries, trying to find them, but they had no luck until one of my colleagues rang them a few hours ago.

"So where were they? Would you care to answer that question... Timothy?"

Timothy Dewdrop looked shocked, horrified even. He looked caught out.

"You said it yourself. You *love* dogs. Like Gordon Gloucester you're an animal lover. When he died you were heartbroken, devastated... Then you found the hyenas in his garage. It wasn't only your father who was there when Gloucester's body was discovered, it was you as well. Before the police or the paramedics or the fire crew arrived you both entered that property. You, Timothy Dewdrop, entered that garage. You found the hyenas and you knew you couldn't leave them there. You had to take care of them, look after them, for the sake of Gordon Gloucester, if nothing else. Your fingerprints were all over the cat cages. You used *them* to spirit away those near harmless baby animals before anybody else knew they were there.

"How did you do this? Nothing more complicated than the boot of your father's car, covered by a mouldy old blanket. The best place to keep them, you thought, was in the crypt of St Blaise's church. You suspected that nobody would find them down there. Who would go down there, into a dank, smelly, disused crypt?

"How were you going to feed them though? You knew they ate meat. You must surely have looked up their diet on the internet. You would have known that hyenas eat almost anything- Flesh, bone, muscle…"

I closed my eyes. I prayed, for a second, that for some reason I wouldn't have to do this.

"Oh, Timothy Dewdrop… What fucked up went through your head? Why did you think it was a good idea to take Gordon Gloucester from his coffin? His coffin which despite the numerous lies pedalled by your father was *not* in the crypt the night before his funeral. Why did you think it was a good idea to take his body from his coffin, replace it with building rubble from a nearby building site, and use it to feed the hyenas?"

"I thought it was what he would have wanted," Dewdrop the Younger confessed. "I thought... I thought he would want to see his animals happy. He wouldn't have wanted them to starve."

"But would he have wanted to be *fed* to them? No. I doubt it. I sincerely doubt it, especially not if he knew that by being fed to those hyenas he would kill them. Gordon Gloucester had been prepared for burial. His body had been pumped full of embalming fluids and chemicals and whatever else it is funeral directors use. The hyenas started to eat, sure… But it wasn't long before they became ill. The poo. The poo that was in the crypt and over the churchyard was the result of the hyena's terrible meal. That was their bodies, shutting down, giving in, reacting to the chemicals.

"And all that, Timothy Dewdrop, would never have been known of had it not been for the jaguar. The escaped jaguar which brought Jessie Hobb to St Blaise's church on the day that Gordon Gloucester was supposed to be buried. Unfortunately for you Mr Hobb has a particularly twisted mind and thought it would be funny to throw the faecal matter about the place. Had he not, had the poo not been there, then Gordon Gloucester's half eaten remains would never have ended up in Crook Street.

"THAT was all for a matter of revenge. Revenge for the throwing of the aforementioned faecal matter. It was because of Hobb being a twisted little mugwort that the next crime happened."

"He deserved it," Dewdrop the Elder leered. "As you say he is a twisted little mugwort. He deserves all of God's wrath and more. I wanted to see him suffer. See him squeal. See him cry and be reduced to…"

"Reduced to a psychotic wreck?"

"He would have been if that dustman hadn't found the body first."

"No. He really wouldn't have been," I said. "Our would be Jeremy Beadle would have filmed it, put it on the internet and turned his millions of adoring acolytes into psychotic wrecks instead. He *did* see the body, Mr Dewdrop, for I showed it to him myself. *He* is the only one who did not almost vomit upon seeing the remains."

"You're all wussies," Hobb smirked.

"No sir we are not wussies. We are rational minded human beings. We have a thing that is known in the business as empathy. We are not desensitised to horrible, disgusting things like you are. Rest assured, you are not alone in lacking empathy. Mr Dewdrop here lacks it also. A man with empathy would not have used the remains of his dead friend to reduce someone to a psychotic wreck, for the sole purposes of revenge."

"If he hadn't thrown the poo I wouldn't have *had* to get revenge," Dewdrop the Elder accused.

"If, if, if… Even an empathetic person would not have gone so far as you did. Perhaps an empathetic person would have restored Gloucester to his coffin, buried the evidence to hide his son's foolish actions. I assume that was the original plan? The coffin was, at that time, still in the church. Gloucester was still to be buried when Hobb showed up. You *claimed* he had been buried that morning, but that was an outright lie. All you had to do was take out the building rubble which Timothy had placed in the coffin, return what was left of Gordon Gloucester, and all would have been buried. You did do that, I think.

"But then along comes Hobb. Already, after finding out

what Timothy has done, you are aggrieved and distraught. How could he? How could he do something so silly? Your own darling son? Then we all know what Hobb did so I won't repeat it. It turns an already bad day into a terrible one. You can't stand it... You snap... You learn who Hobb is thanks to Mr Spicks here and you decide to bring him down. You decide to bring him down and the foolish actions of your own son provide you with the perfect opportunity."

"He deserved it," Dewdrop again claimed.

"Doesn't your son deserve the same?" Parsons ripped. "Isn't feeding someone to a hyena worse than *anything* Jess has done? Shouldn't someone take revenge on him for it? Should I throw him into the jaguar pen back there?"

"That's quite enough Mr Parsons. Debates over the hypocrisy of Mr Dewdrop can wait for another day.

"Your revenge, Mr Dewdrop... Convoluted? Perhaps, but only because you tried to cover your tracks. You tried to disguise yourself, make it look like Gordon Gloucester had led Hobb to his own body."

"I thought it would be... Ironic," Dewdrop confessed. "Imagine, the would be Jeremy Beadle brought to heel from beyond the grave. It was so poetic that I couldn't resist!"

"So you wrapped the remains in the same rag that had been used to cover the cat cages. We found hyena hair on it, just so you know... You, as executor of Gloucester's estate, went into his house, accessed his twitter account from his computer and later tweeted to Mr Hobb a hint that he should go to Crook Street. You then put what was left of Gloucester in the boot of his own car, drove out to Crook Street. You left the car and body there. You knew we would check CCTV to see when the body was dumped and so you thought you would disguise your actions by leaving the car nearby so you could dump the body without being seen. You almost succeeded... You left the car on Crook Street, returned in the middle of the night, using the darkened rows as cover from CCTV, and dumped the body. Unseen, unnoticed, unobserved! You would return the following day for Gloucester's car and hoped that nobody would notice. If you were lucky another car would come down Crook Street in the dead of night and that driver would get the blame. That didn't happen.

"You may have gotten away with it were it not for the fact that you were unbelievably bad at covering your tracks. You *were* caught on CCTV, just not where you thought you would be. You were caught, covered in blood, at the end of Watergate Street. You were seen in a shop, buying milk which we found in Gloucester's fridge. The receipt for that milk was in the bin. It also showed that whoever bought the milk had also bought cigarettes. As Hobb's video in the churchyard betrays, *you* are a smoker. Your fingerprints were all over Gloucester's car, under which the ground was damp. A sure sign that it had recently been AWOL from its drive. There was a glass of brandy by the sink of Gloucester's kitchen. Again your fingerprints were all over it. Your fingerprints were all over Gloucester's keyboard. Gloucester's sat-nav had been programmed for Crook Street. There were bits of Gloucester still in the boot. Best of all was the evidence given to us by Mr Hobb, given to us in the midst of yet another moronic crime. He breached his bail conditions and uploaded the video of him throwing the poo, the very act which spawned your revenge."

What a sorry bunch they were. Dewdrop the Younger, on the verge of tears, sorry for himself and for the foolish, horrible thing he had done. Andrew Parsons, glum faced, perhaps mulling over the idea that he should have been a better parent and that he should have exerted more control over his son. Isherwood Spicks, ashamed, broken, never again to pick up a camera. Jessie Hobb, stone faced, pouty, not sorry about what he had done but sorry that he had been caught. He was eyeing daggers at Dewdrop the Elder, who sat, eyes blazing, furious, angry, righteous. There was no guilt there. There was pride, there was glee. Like Hobb he wasn't sorry for what he had done. He'd do it all over again if he had the chance.

"I suppose now we'll all go to prison?" Dewdrop the Elder mocked.

"You will... But this lot? I shouldn't think so. Mr Parsons won't receive any punishment from the law but he'll have to live the rest of his life with the guilt of not reining his son in when he had the chance. Mr Spicks? As Hobb's accomplice he'll only get a suspended sentence. It may even be reduced because he came in voluntarily."

"Squealer," Hobb spat at him.

"You, Jeremy Beadle, are destined to spend the next few years in a young offender's institute. You can forget about ever uploading another video to the internet because the judicial service will be watching you to make sure you don't."

"And me?" Dewdrop the Younger asked quietly.

"Again, a young offender's institute. At least for the time being. I don't know how long you'll get or what charge they'll give you. Animal neglect as a minimum."

"Improper disposal of a body," Parsons scoffed.

"Maybe. Unlike the US we don't have many laws regarding corpses. Gordon Gloucester had yet to be buried, so you, Timothy Dewdrop, are not going to be charged with body snatching. Conspiring to prevent a lawful burial? Yes, actually. Now that I think on it that will be the likely charge.

"The same will go for Mr Dewdrop the Elder there. You'll be charged with conspiring to prevent a lawful burial as well as improper disposal of a body, conspiracy to pervert the course of justice, exposing a body in a public place, and aggravated conspiracy against a minor…"

"How long will they give me? Two years?"

"Given the seriousness and number of your crimes? I'd say twelve years minimum. You may even get a life sentence if the judge is in a bad mood."

"I see."

He stood up and rolled his sleeves, then he came and stood toe to toe with me. Threatening.

"You are a sick and twisted man, Mr Dewdrop. You always have been. Foisting your own righteous snobbery onto others. But you're no better than the people you look down on. You're no better than Hobb. In fact, you're worse. You think that what you do is absolutely right-on and yet you do things just as terrible. Your righteous sneering is an excuse, a way to pardon your behaviour. It is exactly the same kind of excuse as Mr Hobb uses. It's exactly the same sort of thing as saying: 'it's just a prank, brah!'"

Before I knew what was happening Dewdrop had tried to swing for me. I ducked. He missed. As I came back to where I was he had started to run for the jaguar enclosure. He was actually going to try and kill himself by getting eaten.

Idiot!

Everybody sat, gobsmacked, whilst I gave chase and grabbed his leg as he started to climb over. He kicked me away and his leg came free. Straight over he went, but there was still one obstacle between him and a death by jaguar. An electric fence.

Dewdrop grabbed the fence with both hands and was sent backwards with a piggy little squeal. He was knocked out and came round just in time to be charged.

I added assaulting a police officer to the list of his crimes.

ONE WEEK LATER

Bright sunshine. Not a cloud in the sky.

I was sat on the steps of the town hall, eating lunch and watching the world go by. I was thinking of something I had seen that morning. For breaching his bail conditions Jessie Hobb had already been placed in a young offender's institute. Since then, however, one final video had been uploaded to his channel. I'm guessing it was a hack because Hobb wouldn't have wanted his last video to be of him being beaten to a bloody pulp on the floor, screaming for mercy whilst some buzz-cutted tearaway repeatedly smashed his face in, repeating: 'it's just a prank brah, it's just a prank.'

That, I am not ashamed to admit, had made me smile.

We reap what we sow. Our actions have consequences

and at the end of the day the bailiff has to collect his dues.

"Mr Proctor?" I looked up see Caroline Faulkner. She was smiling, looking ravishing in the sunshine, or as ravishing as one can look given she was wearing a big puffy jacket and carrying a raft of bags. "I asked at the desk, they told me you'd be out here."

"Doctor Faulkner! What can I do for you today?"

"I remembered you saying something about your Gladstone mug being broke so I…" She began rooting through her bags, nearly dropped some of them. I got up to help. "I was in Stoke over the weekend, you see, and… Yes, here it is!" She pulled a cardboard box out of a black bag. Intrigued, I opened it up to find a brand new, grumpy Gladstone face leering out at me through bubble wrap. I was near flabbergasted.

"Thank you. This is wonderful! How much I do I owe you?"

"No charge. I bought a batch of new ones and thought you might like that one."

"Yes! It's lovely… Thank you… But I have to repay you somehow…"

"It's no bother, really."

"Perhaps dinner?" I suggested on the fly. "There's a place the other side of the border if you fancy it. In Trevelyn... My treat?" Faulkner blushed, surprised.

"Oh yes... That would be splendid. I'd love to. When would you like... Oh, I think your sergeant wants you." Gershwin was indeed waving at me from the corner of the building.

"I tell you what... I have your number, I'll call you to arrange a date, yes? Thank you again for the mug."

I hurried off before she could say another word, not because I didn't want her to but because Gershwin had her business face on.

"We've got a weird one sir... Old man holding up a petrol station with a banana."

"Oh happy day!" I rolled my eyes. At least this one wouldn't involve hyena poo or imaginary jaguars.

"What did Faulkner want?" I showed her the mug, a grin on my face, and she pulled a face that was similar to that on the mug. Then, as we climbed into my car, she became mocking.

"I guess love is in the air then? I said that you fancied her."

"I never denied it. I'm taking her for a meal the other side of the border."

"The other side of the border? It must be serious! Speaking of love, how are things with Corwen and Carla?"

"I'm worried," I admitted. "Corwen has agreed to stick around for the sake of Felinheli but I'm beginning to think that he or she was no accident."

"How do you mean?"

"I think Carla *planned* to get pregnant. She was round for lunch on Sunday… There was something about the way she was acting, the way she spoke… I don't think Corwen can see it but if it's true, and it comes out, there might be sparks. Carla is exactly the type to plan an accidental pregnancy."

"Are they really going to call it Felinheli?"

"Aye. Felinheli Naismith-Proctor. I'd have gone for Gwydion myself, but it isn't my choice."

"Both of them sound ridiculous if you ask me," Gershwin said as she began flicking through my CD slipcase.

"I've got a loverly bunch of coconuts," I said out loud.

"Excuse me?"

"I've got a loverly bunch of coconuts… Imogen Virginia

Elaine Gershwin Ophelia Tiffany Abigail Louisa Olive Victoria Eileen Rebecca Laura Yasmin Blossom Ursula Nadine Colette Hephzibah Oriana Francine Catherine Orchid Clara Offenbach Nelly Una Tabitha Smith!"

"My father was a clown," Gershwin grimaced. "He wanted to give me a long name with ridiculous initials. My mother protested and lost. Now please promise me you'll never mention it again?"

"Of course!"

"Excellent. Now how about we deal with this old man and his banana?" She pulled a CD from the slip case and flashed it in the air, grinning. "Whitney?"

"Whitney," I grinned back.

THE MILTON KEYNES
CONSPIRACY

"You were the last person to see Kevin St Claire alive. Please report to Upton Station at once."

I tossed the missive over my shoulder and into the waste paper basket. Had I even heard of Kevin St Claire? I racked my brains, staring at but not reading the report on my desk. The thick one about the right-wing gang which had been keeping me busy for the previous week.

"Gershwin!" I stuck my head around my office door. The only denizen of the office looked up from her magazine, which she had just settled back into after handing me the missive. "Who the fuck is Kevin St Claire?"

A nonchalant shrug. If I had been in a bad mood that shrug would have been insubordination directed at a superior.

"Put it another way. Do we *know* him?"

"Never heard of him until I got that phone call. I knew a Kevin Townsend once."

"Not the same person is it?"

"Marriage?"

"Was he gay?"

"Yes."

"Not LIKELY to be the same person."

Whoever Kevin St Claire was I would gladly declare my ignorance and if someone was trying to add another notch to their "make your own maverick detective" scoreboard then I would shove a chisel up them. They'd already given me a "strong and independent" female sidekick in the form of Gershwin, who I didn't mind much, and that was as far as I was allowing it to go. If I let it carry on they'd be giving me a "genius" nemesis and arranging to have me shot one day before retirement. I wasn't letting them add "suspect in a murder inquiry" to the list.

I decided to make them wait. Figured that with only an hour left on duty I'd visit on my way home. Stop off at the Tesco and the T.K Maxx on the way there. I wanted new clothes for my…

I had a bad feeling they were about to cancel my annual leave and with it my holiday to South Africa. Caroline would be cheesed about that. We'd spent ages haggling to get the same leave. It's the sort of thing they do to maverick detectives.

A stop off at the B&Q to inspect the sharp implements aisle wouldn't exactly go amiss then.

Upton CID was empty apart from two gormless, promoted ahead of their abilities officers. Only ones who had turned up for the evening shift I guessed. Wasn't there a UKIP rally in Warrington tonight? Must have been where the rest of them were. Officers at Upton made no secret of their political allegiances. They gave an uncomfortable truth to the slander of "fascist pigs."

"What's this about Kevin St Claire?"

There was a slow, sluggish movement across a desk, and a file flung across the room like a frisbee. Lucky no papers came out of it. I couldn't help feeling that I was getting the usual "City Centre Cop Contempt" treatment. Or maybe it was because my partner was openly campaigning for Labour in the local council elections.

Easing myself into an empty chair, then moving to rest my feet on the nearest desk, for the purposes of maximum irritation, I pulled out the first sheet.

It looked like a briefing document from Special Branch.

JAMES MORFA

THE MILTON KEYNES KIDNAPPERS
(FOR INTERNAL EYES ONLY)

In the previous five weeks nine men have been abducted from their homes in the middle of the night. Three have been in Lancashire (Blackpool, Morecambe and Worton), two in Yorkshire (Both in Bradford, on successive evenings), one in Cumbria (Barrow-In-Furness) and the remaining three in Lincolnshire (Silbury). There appears to be no connection between the men, nor in the details of the kidnappings apart from that the men were abducted from their homes in the middle of the night, and that a different number with the word: Milton Keynes was left at the sight of the kidnapping. We assume that Milton Keynes is where the hostages have been taken, but so far attempts to trace the kidnappers, including the vehicles and the methods they are using, has yielded no results.

The latest 'victim' is Ephraim Crosby, of Barrow-In-Furness. A delivery driver for BAE systems who was kidnapped in front of his heavily pregnant wife. Crosby's wife has yet to be interviewed as she remains in a critical condition. The number 3 was found pinned to Crosby's pillow by detectives investigating the kidnapping.

HELL! HORROR! To be kidnapped in the dead of night and taken to Milton Keynes? What sadistic bastards would do such a thing?

Naturally, that might not be the case. That could have been misdirection, something the kidnappers found funny. Where's the most random place you can think of? You can't get much more random than Milton bloody Keynes.

I read through the rest of the file- All details about Kevin St Claire. St Claire was apparently based here. I'd seen him at the front desk a couple of times I'd been in for various reasons, I remembered. Not being based here I wouldn't have been able to name him. He was, according to one paper, a twenty three year old athletic type with a husband and a surrogate baby on the way- Gershwin had been weirdly right about the gay marriage thing, but the husband, Gary, had taken St Claire's surname. The surrogate baby was a possible connection. Did the other hostages have babies on the way? Other than that, there was no obvious reason why somebody would want to kidnap these people.

According to a report on his disappearance he had left the station at 18:30 the previous evening and (I had no memory of this) he'd greeted me as I was coming into the reception and he was going out. Racking my brain I remembered that evening I had come in to drop a requested report off and promptly left again. Not a reason to haul me up here. I couldn't recall passing anybody. St Claire must have passed half a dozen people on his way out.

According to the husband's statement he'd never arrived home- Only two streets away from myself, apparently.

"Has anybody called the hospital to see if Kevin St Claire was admitted?"

No answer.

"Have there been any serious traffic accidents reported in the last twenty four hours?"

No answer.

"Listen... If you can't be arsed doing your job why didn't you join the other racists in Warrington?"

Derisive sniffs.

Something was bugging me. I went back to the initial report. No evidence out of nine kidnappings? That seemed unlikely. Wouldn't something like this be national news?

This would be a media sensation. Why hadn't I heard anything about it?

And this business with Kevin St Claire didn't fit the pattern. He'd been kidnapped on his way home in the early evening, not in the dead of night. The county thing wasn't too much of a stretch. They'd already taken from four others, but he was the first from Cheshire. I was dubious of any connection to this Milton Keynes thing anyway- This could have been a standard disappearance, nothing to do with any so called Milton Keynes Kidnappers. I began to think that Upton CID were so feckless that they'd seen the initial report, noticed the disappearance, then put two and two together and got twenty two.

There was a fly buzzing around the neighbouring desk. Somebody had left a plastic packet of fruit salad there and the fly, one of those really tiny annoying things, was taking advantage of the free meal. I watched it and drummed my fingers against the arm of the chair, noting that every so often it jumped from the fruit salad and onto a flyer for a certain racist group I had been investigating. I decided, after thinking of nothing in particular for a while, that the occupant of the desk must have left in a hurry. A crime to solve maybe. More likely a racist rally to get to.

They'd left anyway.

A thought occurred to me.

"How do you lot usually clock in and out of the building?" There were surprised and confused looks from the two layabouts.

"There's a sign in book," one of them said.

"Excellent. And where is it?"

"By the..."

"Go on!"

"By the custody desk at the side entrance."

"Great. So, last night why did Kevin St Claire leave the building by the front entrance?"

Gilbert and his subordinate nephew Jefferson ran the Upton custody desk. They were also in charge of the cells and general station security. Gilbert must have been eighty and Jefferson had about as many brain cells. I caught them as they were about to clock off for the evening and Gilbert wasn't happy.

"Do you have the security tapes for yesterday evening?" I asked politely.

"They can't leave my care you know, and I'm about to go." I tried to be polite.

"This is important. Kevin St Claire. You know him?"

"Course I knows him. Had enough of hearing about him today. Had to get the Chief Super the reception desk tape from yesterday. Got asked about him. Can't say I ever spent any time with him other than remanding."

"Did the chief super only ask for the reception desk tape?"

"Yup."

You'd think a Chief Super Intendant would have better things to do with his time than check footage of a missing police officer. That's the sort of business usually left to the lackeys. You'd also assume they'd have the sense to check the front entrance as well.

"Then I want to see the front entrance tape… AND the reception desk tape."

I could feel something rotten stirring in the pit of my stomach as Gilbert grumbled and brought the tapes out.

"You can ask for copies you know? That's what the Chief

Super did."

"When I've seen the originals I might."

More grumbling from Gilbert followed. I was shown into his back room to see the footage.

It was straight forward. Kevin St Claire crossed the reception area, doffed his hat in greeting to a handsome superior police officer of advancing years coming the other way (I vaguely remembered this now), and vanished out of the front door. Outside he ran to a vehicle on the pavement, smirk on his face, got in, and it sped away. Somebody else, who couldn't be seen, was driving.

I reached for my phone.

"Gershwin... I want a vehicle check. Registration Alpha Papa Victor Nine One One."

"The car belongs to Kevin St Claire," Gershwin replied moments later.

Was that so? Interesting... No. Not interesting.

Fascinating!

An idea came to me.

"May I see the sign in book please?" Gilbert looked like he had been hit in the stomach.

Your average criminal is not a mastermind or a genius or in any way competent at covering up their misdeeds. Most of the time they are blatantly inept. So I was not surprised when I found Kevin St Claire's car parked up his driveway.

"Where's your husband Mr St Claire?" I asked as soon as his husband, Gary, had opened the door. Before he had a chance to see my warrant card. "If you tell me I won't press charges for filing a false report. You picked him up outside Upton Police Station at 6:30 yesterday evening but this morning you claimed he didn't come home last night. So where is he? Mind if I come in?"

I pushed past him without waiting for an answer.

This was a tastefully decorated family home. Good Ikea furniture. A few books. Photographs of the happy couple. No wedding photos though. One of those ultrasound scan photos on the coffee table. Absent mindedly, I picked the latter up, getting lost in a memory of attending Anna's twelve week scan and not being able to tell if we were having a baby or an Illuminati conspiracy. The date of the scan, and the name of the mother, was a revelation.

"When is it due?" I asked, making conversation, pretending I hadn't noticed the date of the scan, then going to take a look in the kitchen. I tested the back door and stuck my head outside to have a look at the garden. It was overgrown and weedy. Full of junk.

"December. We decided on a Christmas baby."

"Cruelty. It'll only get one set of presents a year... Now. Their father. Their... OTHER father. Spill." We returned to the lounge.

"He... You've heard of the Milton Keynes Kidnappers?"

"Yes!" I sat down in an armchair and folded my arms together. "You're either going to tell me he's one of them or he's gone after them."

"We're both part of it. Part of the group." Confessing? Straight away? Alright then...

"The group?"

"It's a police group. I'm based at Wrexham..."

"So you're part of a group of policemen who are kidnapping people and taking them to Milton Keynes?"

I had to pinch myself to stop myself from bursting into giggles at the ludicrousness of this.

"Yes. We have policemen in stations across the country. They identify targets and skew the evidence to hide the crime." I decided to play his little game, to see where it led. Probably to Kevin St Claire, lurking on the staircase with a night stick, waiting for his partner to finish coating the carpet in the legendary baked beans of total bollocks.

"Not hiding the crime very well are you? Special Branch has hold of it, and as soon as you get into an interrogation room the whole conspiracy will be plastered all over the walls. Where abouts in Milton Keynes are you holding them?" There was a long pause.

"It's a dilapidated abbatoir on the outskirts of town."

"Where I assume you put the hostages on meat hooks and torture them? Don't answer that. Do continue though. Why are you doing this? Why are you choosing these particular hostages?"

Gary St Claire paused, trying to think.

"They're… Liberals."

"I'm sorry? LIBERALS?" Gary St Claire tried to backtrack. It was clear from his face that he had slipped up. Give them enough questions, they all do eventually.

"Well… Not Liberals… Errr… Politically correct types…

No… Shit… European Union loving…"

"Stop right there," I said calmly. I had been shown the veneer, a crack in the wrapping paper. It was enough. "There's no such thing as The Milton Keynes Kidnappers. This is all *bullshit*."

There was an eerie, cold silence, a frightened and angry glare.

"First of all, I'd like to know *why*? This whole shit-show was for my benefit I assume? Making sure I was the last one to allegedly see your husband alive? Only I wasn't, was I? You see, I checked the sign in book and your husband signed off duty at 18:15 yesterday evening. Gilbert more or less confessed to that. Then I am assuming he waited until I came by to drop off the report. You knew I was going to do that because you and your husband had sent the request. Standard CID report request. Forged, naturally. I thought nothing of it. Why should I? But the intent… YOUR intent… Was to make sure I was there to be the last person to see Kevin St Claire alive."

"It worked," Gary St Claire sneered.

"It did… And this morning you reported your husband missing." I noticed that every time I referred to Kevin St

Claire as *your husband* Gary's eyes twitched. "Since I was the last person to see your husband alive, I would naturally be called into Upton CID to answer questions, once the tapes from yesterday evening had been checked of course." I paused. "Or were they? You see, Gilbert said something else very interesting. Apparently the Chief Super Intendant checked the tapes personally. Now you're a police officer. Do you think Chief Super Intendant Rotherhithe has the time to watch security footage of a missing constable?"

"He might do…"

"And how intelligent do you think Chief Super Intendant Rotherhithe is? Because Gilbert said something else. Super Intendant Rotherhithe only checked the reception footage, not the front entrance. Surely as a Chief Super Intendant he'd have the intelligence to check the front entrance cameras? But you <u>knew</u> I'd check all the footage, that I'd come here and you could give me your bullshit about being part of the Milton Keynes Kidnappers, about there being a police conspiracy. Then I assume you were going to double down on that. Cosh me over the back of the head, take me to a warehouse somewhere. Make me *think* you really were kidnappers and that there really was a national conspiracy going on. Unfortunately for you, only an idiot would fall for that sort of bullshit, and I am no idiot."

From upstairs there was a roar and a cry and the sound of a body being thrown against the furniture.

"That will be my D.S arresting your husband, who I assume *was* due to cosh me over the head any moment now. Oh, I left the back door open by the way. Hope you don't mind. Anyway, where was I? Ah yes. The Milton Keynes Kidnappers. Admittedly the story had a realm of plausibility to it initially. The report from Special Branch looked authentic enough and it doesn't take a stretch of the imagination to know that there are types out there who do kidnap people in the middle of the night. Mostly people who've been up to their necks in gang related shit. But the more I thought about it the more fanciful it became. More like something out of a detective novel. A bad one at that. The number on the pillow? HA! The lack of evidence? From nine kidnappings? You're telling me that Special Branch can't trace a kidnapping from Barrow-In-Furness, a place that only has ONE MAIN ROAD going in and out? Total horseradish, Mr St Claire.

"And I'll admit I'm baffled as to the purpose of it all, or

why it was me you chose. So, would you care to explain?"

"We wanted you to investigate the conspiracy. We wanted you and your lib-tard station discredited."

"We? Yourself? Your husband? Gilbert? Others at Upton? Those two CID officers who were on duty tonight? Let's say I had fallen for it. How long before I figured out it was all nonsense? I'd say as long as it took me to look up the details of the nine suspects. All of whom I'm guessing were invented?" Gary St Claire looked bitter, twisted. He hadn't expected me to unravel his ridiculous, childish game so quickly.

"So you wanted to get me out of the way. Why? Why did you and *your husband* want me out of the way?"

That last *your husband* almost broke Gary St Claire. His voice took on a nasty edge.

"You… Fucking old liberal woke-tard! We've had enough of the likes of you poncing about, telling us how to think. We're taking this country back. We're taking back control. We'd have had you had laughed off the police force. Early retirement for going crazy, rambling on about kidnappers who don't exist. Not all there anymore. Following ghosts! Believing you'd been kidnapped and trying to blame people for being involved in a conspiracy!"

I almost cracked up. He and his friends at Upton had invented a crazy conspiracy to make *me* look crazy, but all it had done was expose them as children.

"I'm sorry... Did I offend you in some way?" I acted all innocent for a moment. "Oh, I get it... The racist gang I've been investigating. You're one of them! YOUR HUSBAND too? And Gilbert? And the CID officers? You're all part of a little racist cabal going on up at Upton and, correct me if I'm wrong here, I've been getting far too close to the truth for your liking? If I were to carry on investigating I'd have exposed you. Well I'm afraid this charade has done that for me."

Gary St Claire decided to remain silent.

"Why are right wing dick heads so fucking stupid?" Gershwin asked, when we had dispatched both our conspirators off to the cells and we were reclined on their sofa and drinking their red wine.

"Well... If they had any degree of intelligence they

wouldn't be right wing dickheads. They'd have more sense. But it isn't their lack of intelligence that's the problem. It's that they assume everybody else is more idiotic than they are. They thought I'd fall for the idea that people were being kidnapped and taken to sodding Milton Keynes. And take this twelve week scan." I handed Gershwin the ultrasound scan.

"This is dated 1991," she said without hesitation. "Mother by the name of Mrs. H St. Claire."

"It's due in December apparently. TEN MONTHS FROM NOW!" Gershwin started to cackle.

"God, what's that going to be? A twenty six year pregnancy? I don't envy the mother!"

"Anyway… They thought that just because *they* would believe something like the Milton Keynes conspiracy then I would too. Wrong. Very wrong. Clearly they hadn't thought it out either because Gary St Claire, if that is his real name, didn't expect me to ask why they chose those particular targets. That one stumped him."

"Investigation 101- What connects the victims? He'd have never made it to Detective Constable."

"The married couple thing was a nice touch though. That

was the most believable part of the scheme, unless you include the longest pregnancy in history. I assume it was to throw me off the scent of their racism. You'll notice, Miss Watson, there's no wedding photos about the house? I'm sure if we examined all of the ones of them as a couple we'd find they were taken within a day or two, or all in the same place. That one there of them kissing above the fireplace? I bet taking that one really stung them. Good!"

"What's it coming too sir, when the cops side with the fascists and the racists?"

"They'd like to see the backs of you and I D.S Gerswhin because we're old fashioned."

"Speak for yourself. I've got twenty years left before I can retire!"

"You know what I mean. I mean in the way we treat the job. We believe in law and justice and fairness. We show the St Claires up for what they are. A bunch of goomba thugs there for the benefit of the right wing nut jobs. How many of them are there in Upton I wonder? They're endemic in the force, Gershwin. It's sad… Because that means that somewhere out there, tonight, perhaps in Milton Keynes, there's a black teenager being beaten up for a crime he didn't commit. It means there's a gay man "falling down the stairs" to the cells. It means an abused wife is being ignored when she calls for help. It means a rape victim is being blamed for the rapists actions. And do you want to know the worst part?"

"Those two are going to get away with this shit?"

"Those two are going to get away with this shit. And their friends too. Because the rot goes right up."

"Are we fighting a losing battle against these bastards then?"

"I hope not D.S Gershwin."

THE THIRD ARROW

"Hey mate," I said to the man masturbating against the alley wall, half in the light which was clawing its way out from the grease encrusted kitchen window of the Chinese. "Beat it and get some help."

This addict, like every other addict, looked at me with a sneer on his deformed lips, his eyes bloodshot and heroin soaked.

"You startin?" A chavvy, half-scouse thing coming from his mouth. His tiny exposed dick flopping uselessly against his trouser leg.

"Yeah. I'm startin'," I pushed backed. "So beat it... And get... some help."

"Who for? You? Coz you're gonna need an ambulance when I'm through with you." He tried to stand but could hardly manage it. I said my thing once more, with feeling...

"Beat it... And... get... some... help!"

I pulled Lara from across my back and held her as though I were about to shoot. I didn't need to load. I really ought not to have drawn her dry in the way I did. I apologised to her later.

It took a long ten seconds for those meth addled eyes to register. I watched them, perversely enjoying myself as he realised what was in front of him. Those eyes near exploded, thought he might be able to take me for a second, then thought better.

He turned tail and half staggered, vomiting, into the street.

"Get help!" I called after him, lowering Lara, but he didn't hear me.

"Hoping to scare him into rehab?" someone asked from the now open side door of the Chinese. I could smell fried food and feel the heat of the kitchens leaking into the night.

Thomlinson's black eyes watched me from behind a lit cigarette.

"It is Halloween," I shrugged.

"Every night is Halloween in this town. Our vampires stalk the streets night and day. Only they don't drink blood. They drink cheap, shitty white lightning and special brew. Our zombies aren't undead but they almost are with all they drug shit they pump into their systems. And our Frankensteins..."

"You mean Frankenstein's creature. At least in this case." I couldn't help smile. "Most people get arsey and say that Frankenstein was the doctor, not the monster... But it depends on your interpretation. Victor Frankenstein was a monster, if you ask me. In this case though, you *do* mean the creature."

"Don't get smart with me kid. You'll see those creatures on every street corner any morning of the week. Fishnets, too much makeup. Cunts like paper bags…"

"You have such a style Thomlinson," I said. Thomlinson adopted a grim, unhappy expression and his voice become more serious, critical even.

"Kid… I don't agree with what you did… But I protected you when you escaped prison. I hid you. I gave you a safehouse. And in return…"

"You asked me to help with this rotten, lawless shit-hole. I know. You didn't tell me it was the Augean stables." He furrowed his brow. Not a classicist, of course. The reference went over his head, but he understood what it was about.

"Everybody knows that Rhyl is a shit hole. I don't know what you expected. You lived in Chester for all of your life. Everybody in Chester knows Rhyl is a shit hole."

"I did. I just didn't know it was *this* bad… No law? No order? Society doesn't exist here..."

"And that's why we have you, Barnard. My old mentor was a man called Vimes and he taught me one very important lesson that I'm going to pass on to you now.

When your first two arrows fail, you try one last time. You reach for the third arrow."

"He was an archer?"

"A cop, and a thumpin' good un. You know what the first two arrows of society are? Law and order. Ask yourself, what do you do when those two arrows fail? What's the third arrow?"

"I've been asking myself a similar question for two years. What do you do when the law won't help you, when there is no law?"

"You reach for the third arrow. The last chance of hitting the target."

"Depends on what kind of a round you're shooting."

"In this town you are the third arrow."

Thomlinson dropped his cigarette to the step of the takeaway and pulled tomorrow's chip paper from inside the door.

"We're down to our last shot."

I saw nothing unusual in what he handed me. It looked ordinary. It looked, weirdly for Rhyl, nice. At least, it looked nice from what I could manage to read in the steamy light of the takeaway. A local doctor was doing something to help the town. He was offering free drug rehab sessions leading up to Christmas and there was going to be some kind of a fundraising bonfire on the beach at Kinmel Bay.

"This looks good for once," I shrugged, "handing the paper back."

"That doctor… Robespierre McCoy… He's not legit."

"With a name like Doctor McCoy? I wouldn't have thought so."

"There's a rumour going round Kinmel nick that he's paid DCSI Murphey to look the other way for something… Murphey, as it happens, has just this week bought himself a new Jaguar." Always with the jaguars!

"So what? What's he looking the other way from?"

"Look at what he's constructing."

I struggled to read what the paper said. All I could manage was the word: "wicker man."

Thomlinson filled in the rest for me and I wondered if that meth addict had slipped one of us something.

"They get away with it that will be the final breakdown of law and order in this town. This is our last shot and we need our third arrow to hit the mark."

"If he's doing what you say he's going to do… You're

going to need more than a third arrow. You're going to need a cohort of archers."

"Then that's your job," Thomlinson told me. "Get a cohort of archers, stop this, and I'll use the madness as an excuse to properly clean the town up... Because it's got so bad that we've ended up with lunatics like McCoy... This is Chester if you'd gotten away with Croft!"

He slammed the takeaway door behind him and I was left in the dark, holding a newspaper I couldn't see, a newspaper that hinted, to those with certain information (like the local DCSI being bribed to look the other way) that Robespierre McCoy was apparently planning to burn away Rhyl's problems in a massive wicker effigy, for all the world to see.

Evidence... I needed hard, cold, evidence. It was no good Thomlinson telling me the DCSI had been bribed. I needed hard proof of that. More than just rumour. And, I thought, were the police in this town so corrupt they'd let all the drug addicts be burned alive?

I know Rhyl was a near hopeless case when it came to law and order, that is why they needed me as Thomlinson's third arrow, but even here such an atrocity seemed a step too far into madness. Only a lunatic would try such a thing. Especially in… No. *That* was too ludicrous to say. McCoy was probably only a deluded do-gooder. I'd briefly look into it, but it would come to nothing.

I decided that Thomlinson had used Halloween night to give me a scare of my own, something to frighten me into doing a better job cleaning up the Augean stables that is Rhyl. I was coming to the conclusion that, like the Augean stables, only a massive flood could clean the place. For Rhyl only the sea breeching the wall of the promenade could wash its sins from the earth.

As I walked home, keeping an eye out for any signs of trouble on the way, I thought to myself, once more, that no third arrow could ever save this town. You'd need an army. One arrow could only ever hold things in for the briefest time.

SIMON PROCTOR & D.S GERSHWIN RETURN IN…

RHYL ACTUALLY

A down and out seaside town, a plague of zombies… And a massive wicker effigy of Carol Vorderman. It will take more than a police officer to sort this mess out. It's going to need the most infamous dynasty North Wales ever produced.

Printed in Great Britain
by Amazon